Her retre

Somehow, faster than ~~~~~~~~~~~~~ l she could move, Octavia fc ~~~~~~~~~~~ robo-harvester, leaning against the mud-encrusted treads. Behind her, on the steep hillside, the tall crystals ignited. Lightning bolts that sparkled like blue spider-webs connected them all, drawing their power together and weaving it into a knot of energy until all the stray threads converged.

Finally, a beacon of sound and light—some sort of giant transmission—speared upward into the sky and far out into space. It was not directed at her at all, but somewhere distant. To something *not human*.

The shock wave knocked Octavia flat, sending her sprawling on the broken ground. She could barely hold on as the pulsing signal rippled and tore through the air.

Out of breath, frantic, she crawled up the treads of the robo-harvester. As she grabbed the door of the armored cab, her head throbbed and her ears rang. She threw herself inside, slammed the door, and collapsed on the seat. She could barely hear anything.

For the moment she felt protected, but not enough. Moving blindly, she started the engine of the enormous vehicle, wheeled it around on its treads, and crunched over the broken ground at top speed, sending rocks and dirt clods flying as she raced across the valley. She had to get back to Free Haven.

Octavia couldn't think straight, could not yet address in her mind what had happened to her brother, what she had seen with her own eyes.

But she knew she had to warn the other colonists.

STARCRAFT™

SHADOW OF
THE XEL'NAGA

GABRIEL MESTA

This book is a work of fiction. Names, characters, places, and incidents are products of the author's imagination or are used fictitiously. Any resemblance to actual events or locales or persons living or dead is entirely coincidental.

ISBN: 978-1-950366-11-8

First Pocket Books printing: July 2001
First Blizzard Entertainment printing: March 2020

10 9 8 7 6 5 4 3 2 1

Cover art by Bill Petras

Printed in China

This one is for
Scott Moesta,
for his expert advice in the
StarCraft arena (we couldn't
have done it without you).
All those long, hard hours
of playing games finally paid off!

And for his wife,
Tina Moesta,
for understanding that sometimes
a guy has to go kick some
alien butt.

SHADOW OF THE XEL'NAGA

CHAPTER 1

AS A SMOTHERING BLANKET OF DARKNESS descended over the town of Free Haven, the rugged settlers scrambled to avoid the storm. Night came quickly on the colony planet of Bhekar Ro, with plenty of wind but no stars.

Pitch-black clouds swirled over the horizon, caught on the sharp mountainous ridge surrounding the broad valley that formed the heart of the struggling agricultural colony. Already, explosive thunder crackled over the ridge like a poorly aimed artillery barrage. Each blast was powerful enough to be detected on several still-functioning seismographs planted around the explored areas.

Atmospheric conditions created thunder slams with sonic-boom intensity. The roar itself was sometimes sufficient to cause destruction. And what the sonic thunder left unharmed, the laser-lightning tore to pieces.

Forty years earlier, when the first colonists had fled

the oppressive government of the Terran Confederacy, they had been duped into believing that this place could be made into a new Eden. After three generations, the stubborn settlers refused to give up.

Riding in the shotgun seat beside her brother Lars, Octavia Bren looked through the streaked windshield of the giant robo-harvester as they hurriedly trundled back to town. The rumble of the mechanical treads and the roar of the engine almost drowned out the sonic thunder. Almost.

Laser-lightning blasts seared down from the clouds like luminous spears, straight-line lances of static discharge that left glassy pockmarks on the terrain. The laser-lightning reminded Octavia of library images she had seen of a big Yamato gun fired from a battle-cruiser in orbit.

"Why in the galaxy did our grandparents ever choose to move here?" she asked rhetorically. More laser-lightning burned craters into the countryside.

"For the scenery, of course," Lars joked.

While the bombardment of hail would clear the air of the ever-present dust and grit, it would also damage the crops of triticale-wheat and salad-moss that barely clung to the rocky soil. The Free Haven settlers had few emergency provisions to help them withstand any severe harvest failure, and it had been a long time since they had asked for outside help.

But they would survive somehow. They always had.

Lars watched the approaching storm, a spark of

excitement in his hazel eyes. Though he was a year older than his sister, when he wore that cocky grin on his face he looked like a reckless teenager. "I think we can outrun the worst of it."

"You always overestimate what we can do, Lars." Even at the age of seventeen, Octavia was known for her stability and common sense. "And I always end up saving your butt."

Lars seemed to have a bottomless reservoir of energy and enthusiasm. She gripped her seat as the big all-purpose vehicle crunched through a trench and continued along a wide beaten path between plantings, heading toward the distant lights of the town.

Shortly after their parents' death, it had been Lars's crazy suggestion that the two of them expand their cultivated land and add remote automated mineral mines to their holdings. She had tried, unsuccessfully, to talk him out of it. "Let's be practical, Lars. We've already got our hands full with the farm as it is. Expanding would leave us time for nothing but work—not even families."

Half of the colonists' eligible daughters had already filed requests to marry him—Cyn McCarthy had filed three separate times!—but so far Lars had made plenty of excuses. Colonists were considered adults at the age of fifteen on this rough world, and many were married and had children before they reached their eighteenth birthday. Next year, Octavia would be facing the same decision, and choices were few in Free Haven.

"Are you sure we want to do this?" she had asked one last time.

"Of course. It's worth the extra effort. And once we're established there'll be plenty of time for each of us to get married," Lars had insisted, shaking back his shoulder-length sandy hair. She had never been able to argue with that grin. "Before we know it, Octavia, it'll all turn around, and then you'll thank me."

He had been certain they could grow crops high on the slopes of the Back Forty, the ridge that separated their lands from another broad basin and more mountains twelve kilometers away. So the brother and sister had used their robo-harvester to scrape flat a new swath of barely arable farmland and plant new crops. They also set up automated mineral mining stations on the rocky slopes of the foothills. That had been almost two years ago.

Now a gust of wind slammed into the broad metal side of the harvester, rattling the sealed windowports. Lars compensated on the steering column and accelerated. He didn't even look tired from their long day of hard work.

Laser-lightning seared across the sky, leaving colorful tracks across her retinas. Though he couldn't see any better than his sister, Lars didn't slow down at all. They both just wanted to get home.

"Watch out for the boulders!" Octavia said, her piercing green eyes spotting the hazard as rain slashed across the windows of the impressive tractorlike vehicle.

Lars discounted the rocks, drove over them, and crushed the stone with the vehicle's treads. "Aww, don't underestimate the capabilities of the machine."

She snorted indelicately. "But if you throw a plate or fry a hydraulic cam, *I'm* the one who has to fix it."

The multipurpose robo-harvester, the most important piece of equipment any of the colonists owned, was capable of bulldozing, tilling, destroying boulders, planting, and harvesting crops. Some of the big machines had rock-crusher attachments, others had flamethrowers. The vehicles were also practical for traversing ten- to twenty-klick distances over rough terrain.

The hull of the robo-harvester, once a gleaming cherry red, was now faded, scratched, and pitted. The engine ran as smoothly as a lullaby, though, and that was all Octavia cared about.

Now she checked the weather scanner and atmospheric-pressure tracker in the robo-harvester's cabin, but the readings were all wild. "Looks like a bad one tonight."

"They're always bad ones. This is Bhekar Ro, after all—what do you expect?"

Octavia shrugged. "I guess it was good enough for Mom and Dad." *Back when they were alive.*

She and Lars were the only survivors of their family. Every family among the settlers had lost friends or relatives. Taming an uncooperative new world was dangerous, rarely rewarding work, always ripe for tragedy.

But the people here still followed their dreams. These exhausted colonists had left the tight governmental fences of the Confederacy for the promised land of Bhekar Ro some forty years before. They had sought independence and a new start, away from the turmoil and constant civil wars among the inner Confederacy worlds.

The original settlers had wanted nothing more than peace and freedom. They had begun idealistically, establishing a central town with resources for all the colonists to share, naming it Free Haven, and dividing farmland equally among the able-bodied workers. But in time the idealism faded as the colonists endured toil and new hardships on a planet that did not live up to their expectations.

Nobody among the colonists ever suggested going back, though—especially not Octavia and Lars Bren.

The lights of Free Haven glowed like a warm, welcoming paradise as the robo-harvester approached. In the distance Octavia could already hear the storm-warning siren next to the old missile turret in the town plaza, signaling colonists to find shelter. Everyone else—at least the colonists who had common sense—had already barricaded themselves inside their prefabricated homes to shelter from the storm.

They passed outlying homes and fields, crossed over dry irrigation ditches, and reached the perimeter of the town, which was laid out in the shape of an octagon. A low perimeter fence encircled the settlement, but the gates for the main streets had never been closed.

An explosion of sonic thunder roared so close that the robo-harvester rattled. Lars gritted his teeth and drove onward. Octavia remembered sitting on her father's knee during her childhood, laughing at the thunder as her family had gathered inside their home, feeling safe . . .

Their grandparents had aged rapidly from the rigors of life here and had the dubious distinction of being the first to be buried in Bhekar Ro's ever-growing cemetery outside Free Haven's octagonal perimeter. Then, not long after Octavia had turned fifteen, the spore blight had struck.

The sparse crops of mutated triticale-wheat had been afflicted by a tiny black smut on a few of the kernels. Because food was in short supply, Octavia's mother had set aside the moldy wheat for herself and her husband, feeding untainted bread to their children. The meager meal had seemed like any other: rough and tasteless, but nutritious enough to keep them alive.

Octavia remembered that last night so clearly. She had been suffering from one of her occasional migraines and a dire sense of unreasonable foreboding. Her mother had sent the teenage girl to bed early, where Octavia had had terrible nightmares.

The next morning she had awakened in a too-quiet house to find both of her parents dead in their bed. Beneath wet sheets twisted about by their final agony, the bodies of her mother and father were a quivering, oozing mass of erupted fungal bodies, rounded mushrooms of exploding spores that rapidly disintegrated all flesh . . .

Lars and Octavia had never returned to that house, burning it to the ground along with the tainted fields and the homes of seventeen other families that had been infected by the horrible, parasitic disease.

Though a terrible blow to the colony, the spore blight had drawn the survivors together even more tightly. The new mayor, Jacob "Nik" Nikolai, had delivered an impassioned eulogy for all the victims of the spore plague, somehow rekindling the fires of independence in the process and giving the settlers the drive to stay here. They had already lived through so much, survived so many hardships, that they could pull through this.

Moving together into an empty prefab dwelling at the edge of Free Haven, Octavia and Lars had rebuilt their lives. They made plans. They expanded. They tracked their automated mines and watched the seismic monitors for signs of tectonic disturbances that might affect their work or the town. The two drove out to the fields each day and labored side by side until well after dark. They worked harder, risked more . . . and survived.

As Octavia and Lars passed through the open gate and drove around the town square toward their residence, the storm finally struck with full force. It became a slanting wall of rain and hail as the roboharvester ground its way past the lights and barricaded doors of metal-walled huts. Their own home looked the same as all the others, but Lars found it by instinct, even in the blinding downpour.

He spun the large vehicle to a halt in the flat gravel clearing in front of their house. He locked down the treads and powered off the engine, while Octavia tugged a reinforced hat down over her head and got ready to jump out of the cab and make a break for the door. Even running ten feet in this storm would be a miserable ordeal.

Before the robo-harvester's systems dimmed completely, Octavia checked the fuel reservoirs, since her brother never remembered to do so. "We'll need to get more vespene gas from the refinery."

Lars grabbed the door handle and hunched his head down. "Tomorrow, tomorrow. Rastin's probably hiding inside his hut cursing the wind right now. That old codger doesn't like storms any more than I do."

He popped open the hatch and jumped out seconds before a strong gust slammed the door back into its frame. Octavia exited from the other side, hopping from the step to the broad tractor treads to the ground.

As she ran beside her brother in a mad dash to their dwelling, the hail hit them like machine-gun bullets. Lars got their front door open, and the siblings crashed into the house, drenched and windblown. But at least they were safe from the storm.

Sonic thunder pealed across the sky again. Lars undid the fastenings on his jacket. Octavia yanked off her dripping hat and tossed it into a corner, then powered up their lights so she could check one of the old seismographs they had installed in their hut.

Few of the other colonists bothered to monitor planetary conditions or track underground activity anymore, but Lars had thought it important to place seismographs in their automated mining stations out in the Back Forty foothills. Of course, Octavia had been the one to repair and install the aging monitoring equipment.

Lars had been right, though. There had been increasing tremors of late, setting off ripples of aftershocks that originated deep in the mountain range at the far side of the next valley.

Just what we need—another thing to worry about, Octavia thought, looking at the graph with concern.

Lars joined her to read the seismograph strip. The long and shaky line appeared to have been drawn by a caff-addicted old man. He saw several little blips and spikes, probably echoes of sonic thunder, but no major seismic events. "Now that's interesting. Aren't you glad we didn't have an earthquake tonight?"

She knew it would happen even before he finished his sentence. Maybe it was another one of Octavia's powerful premonitions, or just a discouraged acceptance that things would get worse whenever they had the opportunity.

Just as Lars formed another of his cocky grins, a tremor rippled through the ground, as if the uneasy crust of Bhekar Ro were having a nightmare. At first Octavia hoped it was merely a particularly close blast of sonic thunder, but the tremors continued to build, lurching the floor beneath their feet and shaking the entire prefab house.

Lars tensed his powerful muscles to ride out the temblor. They both watched the seismograph go wild. "The readings are off the scale!"

Astonished, Octavia pointed out, "This isn't even centered *here*. It's fifteen klicks away, over the ridge."

"Great. Not far from where we set up all our automated mining equipment." The seismograph went dead, its sensors overloaded, as the quake pounded the ground for what seemed an eternity before it gradually began to fade. "Looks like you're gonna have some repair work to do tomorrow, Octavia."

"I've always got repair work to do," she said.

Outside, the storm reached a crescendo. Lars and Octavia sat together in weary silence, just waiting out the disaster. "Do you want to play cards?" he asked.

Then all the lights inside their dwelling went out, leaving them in pitch blackness lit only by flares from the laser-lightning.

"Not tonight," she said.

CHAPTER 2

THE QUEEN OF BLADES.

Her name had once been Sarah Kerrigan, back when she'd been something else . . . back when she'd been human.

Back when she'd been *weak*.

She sat back within the pulsing organic walls of the burgeoning zerg hive. Monstrous creatures moved about in the shadows, guided by her every thought, functioning for a greater purpose.

With her mental powers and her control over these awful and destructive creatures, a transformed Sarah Kerrigan had established the new hive on the ashen ruins of the planet Char. It was a gray world, blasted and still smoldering from potent cosmic radiation. This planet had long been a battlefield. Only the strongest could survive here.

The vicious zerg race knew how to adapt, how to survive, and Sarah Kerrigan had done the same to become one of them. Raised as a psi-talented ghost, a telepathically powered espionage and intelligence agent for the Terran Confederacy, she had been captured by the zerg Overmind and transformed.

Her skin, toughened with armor-polymer cells, glowed an oily, silvery green. Her yellow lambent eyes were surrounded by dark patches of skin that could have been bruises or shadows. Her hair had become Medusa spines—jointed segments like the sharp legs of a venomous spider. Each spike writhed as plans continuously burned through her brain. Her face still had a delicate beauty that just might lull a human victim into a moment of hesitation—giving her enough time to strike.

When she caught a reflection of herself, Sarah Kerrigan occasionally recalled what it had been like to be human, to be lovely—in a human sort of way— and that she had once even begun to love a man named Jim Raynor, who was also very much in love with her. *Human emotions and weaknesses.*

Jim Raynor. She tried not to remember him. She would have no scruples now against killing the burly, good-natured man with his walrus mustache, if such was required of her. She did not regret what had happened to her, since she had a more important mission now.

Sarah Kerrigan was much more than just another zerg.

The various zerg minions had been adapted and mutated from other species that they had infested during their history of conquest. Drawing from a sweeping catalog of DNA and physical attributes, the zerg could live anywhere. The swarms were as much at home on bleak Char as they had been on the lush terran colony world of Mar Sara.

A truly magnificent species.

The zerg swarm would sweep across the worlds in the galaxy, consuming and infesting every place they touched. Because of their nature, the zerg could suffer overwhelming catastrophic losses and still keep coming, keep devouring.

But in the recent war against the protoss and the Terran Confederacy, the almighty Overmind had been destroyed. And *that* had nearly spelled the end for the zerg.

At first, their victory had seemed secure as the zerg infested the two terran fringe colony worlds of Chau Sara and Mar Sara. Their numbers grew while the rest of the Confederacy remained oblivious to the danger. But then a protoss war fleet—never before seen by humans— had sterilized the face of Chau Sara. Though the unexpected attack obliterated the zerg infestation there (and also slaughtered millions of innocent human colonists), the Terran Confederacy had responded immediately to this unprovoked aggression. The protoss commander had not had the will to destroy the second world of Mar Sara, and so the zerg infestation grew there unchecked.

Eventuallly, the zerg minions had wiped out the Terran Confederate capital of Tarsonis. And Sarah Kerrigan, human ghost, a covert psi-powered operative, had been betrayed by her fellow military comrades and infested by the zerg. Recognizing her incredible telepathic powers, the Overmind had decided to use her for something special . . .

But then, on the nearly conquered protoss home planet of Aiur, a protoss warrior had killed the Overmind in a suicidal explosion that made a hero of him and decapitated the zerg hive.

Leaving Sarah Kerrigan, the Queen of Blades, to pick up the pieces.

Now the control of the vicious, swarming race lay in her clawed hands. She faced the tremendous challenge of transforming the planet into a new nexus for the perfect zerg race. The swarms would rise again.

Under her guidance, a few surviving drones had metamorphosed into hatcheries. Kerrigan's zerg followers had found and delivered enough minerals and resources to convert those hatcheries into more sophisticated lairs . . . and then into complete Hives. Before long, the organic mat of zerg creep spread over the charred surface of the planet. The nourishing substance offered food and energy for the various minions of the new colony.

It was everything she needed to restore the wounded, but never defeated, zerg race.

Kerrigan sat surrounded by the light. Her mind wasfilled with details reported to her by the dozens of surviving overlords, huge minds that carried separate swarms on missions dictated by their Queen of Blades. She did not relax, she never slept. There was too much work to do, too many plans to lay . . . too much revenge to achieve.

Sarah Kerrigan flexed her long-fingered hands, extended the rapier-like claws that could disembowel an opponent—*any opponent*, from the treacherous rebel Arcturus Mengsk, who had betrayed her, to General Edmund Duke, whose ineptitude had led to her eventual capture and transformation.

She looked down at one claw, thinking of how she could draw it across the throat of the jowly iron-edged general and watch his fresh hot blood spill out. Though they had not intended it as a favor, Edmund Duke and Arcturus Mengsk had made it possible for her to become the Queen of Blades, to reach the full power and fury of her potential. How could she be angry with them for that?

Still . . . she wanted to kill them.

In the hive around her, zerglings moved about, each the size of a dog she had once owned as a young girl. They were insect-shelled creatures shaped like lizards, with clacking claws and long fangs. Zerglings were fast little killing machines that could descend like piranha onto an enemy army and tear the soldiers to pieces.

Sarah Kerrigan found them beautiful, just as a mother would view any of her precious children. She stroked the gleaming greenish hide of the nearest zergling. In response, it ran its claws over her own nearly indestructible skin, then dusted her with the feathery touch of its fangs, a caress that might have been fondness . . .

Hideous hydralisks patrolled the perimeter of the colony, some of the most fearsome of the zerg minions. Flying, crablike guardians soared overhead, ready to spew acid that would destroy any ground-based threat.

The zerg swarm was safe and secure.

Sarah Kerrigan wasn't worried, and certainly not afraid, but she was careful. She moved about restlessly on powerful muscles, though she could see everything through the eyes of her minions if she chose.

Along with her remaining human ambition and the emotional sting of betrayal, she also felt the relentless conquering urge that came from her new zerg genetics.

In aeons long past, the mysterious and ancient race of the xel'naga had created the zerg race, their perfect design relentless and pure. Kerrigan smiled at the delicious irony of it. The zerg had been so perfect they had eventually turned on their creators and infested the xel'naga themselves.

Now that the leadership of all the swarms was in her own hands, Kerrigan promised herself that she would lead the zerg to the pinnacle of their destiny.

But when she sat back in her hive and watched the swarming creatures going about their business, gathering resources and preparing for war, the Queen of Blades felt the tiniest remnant of human sympathy stirring in her heart.

She felt sorry for *anyone* who got in her way.

CHAPTER 3

AS IF TAUNTING THEM WITH THE WEATHER'S capriciousness, the next morning on Bhekar Ro dawned bright and clear. It reminded Octavia of the photo-images the original survey crew had shown her grandparents to lure them and the first group of desperate settlers here.

Maybe it wasn't all lies after all . . .

As she and Lars cracked open the door seal of their dwelling, a trickle of rainwater ran down from the entryway, pattering onto the soft ground. High overhead, the angular shape of a glider hawk cruised along, searching for the flooded-out bodies of drowned lizards.

Octavia trudged across the drying muck to the robo-harvester. With a shake of her short brown curls, she set to work. She ran an experienced eye over the hull and noticed dozens of new hail craters pounded into the metal, making it look like the rind of a sourange. Of course, nobody on Bhekar Ro cared much about shiny paint jobs, as long as the equipment worked. She was relieved to find that the storm had done no serious damage to the machinery.

Up and down the town streets, ragged colonists woke up and emerged from their houses to assess the damage, as they had done so many times before. From a nearby dwelling, Abdel and Shayna Bradshaw were already squabbling, dismayed at the amount of repair work they would have to do. From across the street Kiernan and Kirsten Warner waved to Cyn McCarthy, who trotted toward the mayor's house at the center of town, an optimistic smile on her freckled face in spite of the disaster. Good-natured Cyn had a habit of offering her help wherever it might be needed, though the copper-haired young woman often forgot to do what she had promised.

Because the rough weather came at unpredictable times, with no identifiable storm season, the settlers had a continuous battle to repair what was broken. They constantly planted the cleared fields, rotating crops from whip-barley to triticale-wheat to salad-moss, hoping to harvest more than they lost, striving to get two steps ahead before they had to take one step back again.

Among the casualties of the devastating spore plague had been four of the colony's best scientists. Cyn McCarthy's husband, Wyl, a second-generation chemical engineer, had been one of them. For the first decades, the scientists had worked with the planet's resources and environment, concocting biological modifications of the crops and animals to increase their chances of survival. Free Haven had been stable for a while, the arable land slowly increasing.

But the deaths of these educated people left the rest of the untrained settlers too busy with simple survival to learn any new specialties. The colonists went about their tasks as farmers, mechanics, and miners, their daylight hours filled with urgent matters that left no time for exploration or expansion. The general consensus, voiced by Mayor Nikolai, was that investigation and scientific pursuits were a luxury they could return to at some later date.

"Any real damage?" Lars asked his sister as she finished her inspection of the big robo-harvester.

Octavia rapped her knuckles on the pitted and scarred door. "A few more scrapes. Just cosmetic."

"Beauty marks. Adds character." Lars opened the door, and melted hailwater ran out of the cab and down through the flat metal treads. "We need to get out to the Back Forty and check on those seismographs and the mining stations. That quake hit them pretty hard."

Octavia smiled, knowing her brother well. "And, since we're out there, you'll want to see if the tremors uncovered anything."

He gave her that grin again. "Just part of the job. We registered some pretty hefty seismic jolts. Could be significant. And you *know* none of the other settlers is going to bother taking a look."

The decades-old weather stations and seismographs

the scientists had set up at the valley perimeter continued to take readings, and occasionally Lars would retrieve the data. For the most part, the settlers stayed within their safe cultivated valley, growing enough food to stay alive, mining enough minerals to repair their facilities, but never expanding beyond their capabilities.

In the past, other colonists had tried to establish settlements beyond the main valley. Some had moved away from Free Haven, searching for better farmland. But one by one each of those distant farms had fallen to blight, plague, or natural disaster, and the few survivors had made their way back to the colony town in defeat.

Octavia climbed aboard the robo-harvester with Lars as he powered up the engines. She swung the door shut just as the thick treads began to move. Other settlers set out in their own vehicles to inspect their fields, clearly anticipating the worst.

Octavia and Lars took the robo-harvester far out toward the foothills. Lars had the true pioneer spirit, always wanting to find new mineral deposits, productive vespene geysers, fertile land. He would be happy just to *make* discoveries, while Octavia hoped to fulfill her parents' dream and actually transform Bhekar Ro into a place where they could be proud to live. Someday.

As the big vehicle trundled across the valley floor, she could see that many of the fragile crops had been hammered by the storm. The hail and sonic thunder had battered tall stalks to the mucky ground or bruised unripened fruit; the laser-lightning had set stunted orchards on fire.

A few hardy farmers were already out trying to salvage what they could. Gandhi and Liberty Ryan, sweating in their overalls, worked hard to erect protective bubbles over the seedlings, assisted by their adopted hand, Brutus Jensen, and three children of their own. The family members were too tired even to talk to one another as they went about their labors. Brutus Jensen managed to give them a half-hearted wave, while the Ryans could barely nod.

Kilometers farther along, the road dwindled to little more than a path marked on a navigation screen. They paused briefly at the far edge of the officially settled area.

Lars kept the robo-harvester's engine running as he called out in the direction of a shack and some storehouses. "Hey, Rastin! Get out of that puttering refinery and hook us up so we can fill our tanks. Or have you been sniffing too much vespene gas?"

The lanky old prospector strode around the hissing and throbbing stations he had built around the cluster of chemical geysers where he had staked his claim. Old Blue, his mastiff-sized dog, came out from his sleeping hole under the corrugated metal porch.

The dog's lips were curled back and his sky-blue fur bristled as he growled, but Octavia climbed out of the robo-harvester and clapped her hands. "You don't fool me, you grouch of a dog."

With a happy bark, Old Blue bounded toward her,

his thick tail wagging. She patted his head and high shoulders, trying unsuccessfully to keep his muddy paws off her jumpsuit.

Rastin and Lars exchanged complaints and insults—because that was the way the old prospector conducted business—but Rastin wasted no time filling up their vehicle. Octavia had never been able to decide whether the codger was an efficient worker or just anxious to get rid of any visitors so he could go back to his solitude.

One of the few surviving original settlers, Rastin had been independent and alone on Bhekar Ro for forty years. He had always wanted to get away from the Terran Confederacy, and might actually have preferred an empty habitable world all his own; the small group on this planet had been the best he could do.

Rastin lived in an often-repaired shack made out of spare components. He had erected his refinery over a cluster of four vespene geysers, one of which was already played out. The remaining trio of geysers produced enough of the fuel to meet the colony's modest needs.

Having fueled the robo-harvester, the old prospector sent them off with a gruff wave that looked very much like a gesture of disgust. Octavia patted Old Blue's big head again before she stepped back up onto the vehicle's muddy treads. The dog bounded off with the grace of a jumping mule as it spotted a hairy rodent dashing between broken rocks.

Rastin went back to tinkering with his equipment,

grumbling because after the earthquake another of the geysers had stopped producing. He delivered a swift kick to the pumping station, but even this tried-and-true repair procedure did not wake the geyser.

Leaving Rastin's homestead, Lars and Octavia ascended into the steep foothills toward the boundary ridge. The terrain became much rougher. Their Back Forty extended far past where the potential cropland had been demarcated by the cooperative families. Out here, the mineral and resource rights had been up for grabs to anyone with the spare time or ambition to increase their acreage. So Lars and Octavia had staked out a claim, in addition to the fields their parents and grandparents had tilled.

As the morning grew warmer and the orange sun climbed into the sky, bleaching away shadows, the robo-harvester clawed up a steep ridge, following paths that only Lars had ever driven. "Our mining stations are still off-line," he said, his voice flat. "And that's the most I can say."

As he brought the robo-harvester to a halt, Octavia could see to her dismay that the automated installations were tilted on their anchor pads, obviously damaged and unable to function.

"Go to it, Octavia—you're the expert."

With a sigh, she descended from the vehicle and hunkered down to see how much repair the mining stations would require. She studied the control panel of the processing turret, surprised at how many red warning lights were illuminated at the same time.

Under normal operation, the clunky machines would wander over the rocky slopes, taking mineral samples and marking desirable deposits. Then processing turrets would be erected so that the mining and extraction activities could continue until a valuable vein had been processed, while the mechanized scout continued to search for more sites.

Lars left his sister to her work. "I'm going up to the top of the ridge to see about those seismographs. Maybe I can fix them myself."

Octavia suppressed a disbelieving snort. "Be my guest."

Her brother climbed up the slope from boulder to boulder, until he topped the saddle and stared across the next valley. She didn't notice how long he stood in silent awe before he started yelling for her. "Octavia! Come up here!"

She looked up, slammed the service door shut on the mining turret, then stood. "What is it?"

But Lars bounded up onto a higher rocky outcropping, from which he could get a better view. He gave a low whistle. "Now *this* is interesting."

Octavia scrambled after him while the back of her mind ran through the different tricks she'd probably have to use to get the mining stations functional again. She knew Lars got distracted easily.

From the top, she got a good look into the next valley, quickly seeing the changes the previous night's earthquake had wrought. Numerous new vespene geysers steamed into the air, curls of silvery-white mist that could provide the colony with more than enough fuel for the next several decades.

But that wasn't what had caught her brother's eye.

"What do you think it is?" He gestured wildly toward the next rugged ridge across the bowl-shaped valley, twelve kilometers from Free Haven.

Before the quake, a prominent conelike peak had jutted into the sky, a distinctive landmark on the continent. But that was yesterday.

The terrible storm and severe tremors had sparked a huge avalanche, breaking off an entire side of the mountain. The stones had fallen away, split off like a scab ripped from a ragged wound, to expose something very strange—and completely unnatural—inside the mountain.

And it was glowing.

The two of them rushed back to the robo-harvester. The big vehicle crunched across the rough terrain and over the mountainous saddle, then toiled headfirst down the easiest switchbacked path into the adjacent valley. Lars drove faster than she had ever seen him try, but Octavia didn't complain. For once, she felt as eager to investigate as her brother did.

He raced past the hissing geysers and clouds of eye-stinging gases, leaving deep tracks in the soft valley floor. Small animals of species Octavia had never seen—they probably weren't edible anyway—scampered out of the way.

Finally, the vehicle crunched to an abrupt stop at

the base of the avalanche field where the mountain-side had collapsed. Octavia peered up through the dusty windshield at an enormous structure. She and Lars both stared at it in fascination and confusion, before jumping simultaneously out of the robo-harvester for a better look.

Neither of them had any idea what the object could be.

Once buried deep within the mountain, the amazing artifact now pulsed like a huge resinous beehive. Its swirled walls and curved faces were lumpy and pocked with open air vents or passages. There seemed to be no functional design, no sensible blueprint, no purpose that Octavia could fathom.

But the thing was obviously of alien origin. Possibly organic.

"I guess we're not alone here on this planet," she said.

CHAPTER 4

THE ABANDONED WORLD HAD NO REMEMBERED name. The planet was so obscure that it did not show up on even the most detailed of protoss charts.

The scholar female Xerana stepped on the dusty, time-worn remnants of what must once have been a xel'naga outpost, probably the first living being to stand here since the ancient progenitors had vanished into history and legend. She marveled at the idea and felt a stab of disappointment that she could never share this with the rest of the protoss race.

Her broad, knobbed feet crunched on tiny pebbles and rubble. No doubt, all of this had been a magnificent city, ages ago. The smell of dust and mystery hung thick in the still air.

Xerana, like the others of the dark templar, had been banished from protoss society, exiled from their beloved homeworld of Aiur. When the protoss judicators had commanded that all members of their race must join the way of the Khala, the telepathic union that connected the protoss in a sea of thought, the dark templar had refused to follow. They became outcasts, persecuted because they feared the Khala would strip away their individuality, melding them into an overall subconscious mind.

Although the stern judicators had driven them off and even now continued to hunt them down, the exiles bore the protoss no ill will. The fabled xel'naga race had created all of them. The followers of the Khala disagreed with the dark templar on fundamental issues, but Xerana and her comrades still considered the Firstborn—the protoss—their brothers and sisters.

And because they strove to better themselves in ways that the other protoss refused to consider, the dark templar had discovered new sources of information. Xerana herself had unearthed many artifacts of the xel'naga and secrets of the Void. The other protoss did not have such things, and they might never learn unless they stopped hating the dark templar . . .

On the silent, haunted landscape, Xerana stepped out under an orange sky and continued to walk among the powdery ruins. Even among the dark templar, she was a loner, a scholar. She was obsessed with finding any information about the ancient race that had created the protoss, and much later the hideous zerg.

But the ruins on this abandoned planet had been worn down by erosion, erasing the most dramatic of remnants. Xerana did not give in to discouragement. She continued to dig.

She looked up, saw a gauze of grayish clouds crawl over the orange sky, and wondered if a storm was coming and if she might be in danger. But the gray clouds, like visual static or smoke, soon dissipated. Xerana bent back to her work, searching the rubble.

As twilight came, she allowed herself to imagine the evening activities that the xel'naga must have enjoyed. She knew the ancients had walked here in the shadows, and she now followed in their footsteps.

The Xel'Naga, also called the "Wanderers from Afar," were a peaceful and benevolent race, driven by the goal of studying and then spreading sentient evolution throughout the universe. After many experiments on other worlds, the xel'naga had come to the jungle world of Aiur and concentrated their efforts on the indigenous race there, secretly guiding them through evolution and civilization until they became the protoss, the Firstborn.

But when the satisfied and triumphant xel'naga finally revealed themselves, they unwittingly caused world-spanning chaos. The protoss tribes split apart, each finding different ways to advance themselves. Some even turned upon the ancient Xel'Naga, finally driving away the Wanderers from Afar and then attacking each other in a protracted and bloody civil war known as the Aeon of Strife.

Eventually, the protoss healed their civilization by bringing the race together in a religious and telepathic bonding known as the Khala. For many centuries, the Khala allowed the protoss to grow strong again, although it engendered a rigid caste system, limited independent thought, and blurred the distinction between individuals. Adherence to the path of the Khala was strictly enforced by unwavering religious-political leaders called judicators.

A few protoss tribes refused the Khala, separating themselves from it and holding to their precious individuality. For a long time, the existence of these rebels remained a dark secret. And then came the persecution, until finally the Judicator Conclave banished all of the rogue Ttribes, placing their members aboard a derelict xel'naga ship and sending them off into the Void.

These exiled rebels had become the dark templar, like Xerana, still loyal to the race that had driven them out but voraciously inquisitive, burning to understand their origins. Xerana needed to know why the xel'naga had considered the protoss failures, why they had never returned, and why they had later devoted their efforts to creating the vicious zerg.

Like the others of her group, Xerana was a warrior as well as a researcher and scholar. So far, she had deciphered a great deal of xel'naga lore. Other dark templar had also tapped into the powers of the Void, learning secret psi techniques that the rest of the protoss race did not understand . . .

Even when darkness fell on this unnamed world, Xerana still did not return to her large ship in orbit.

Her golden gemfire eyes adapted to the dark, her telepathic senses extended, and she continued to search. Her slender, muscular body was covered by dark robes held in place by a wide hieroglyphic-inscribed sash that signified her scholar's profession. She wore her clothing as a matter of formality and function, never for comfort. Affixed to her wide collar was a thin, etched tablet, a fragment she had found on an earlier excavation, displaying indecipherable words that had been inscribed by the hand of a long-forgotten xel'naga poet. It was her most prized possession.

Traveling farther, Xerana found broken pillars, weathered columns of stone that time had polished smooth. She could make out the arrangement, though, similar to that of temples she had seen on other worlds. The pillars of rock had been placed in a precise pattern, as if to focus the energies of the cosmos.

The columns had slumped under the weight of ages, battered by cosmic rays and pounding heat, scoured by millennia of wind that, on this world of unexpected colors, was as faint as a baby's breath. All around her in this place, Xerana could sense their presence with her psionic powers. She felt the whispers acknowledging her, guiding her.

She kicked over a crumbling boulder on impulse, and there, underneath the protective barrier of rock, saw a curved light stone, facedown in the ashy earth.

Ah . . .

Xerana pried it up and found a small fragment of an obelisk. A few faint pictographs still remained on the weathered and burned chunk of stone. This was what she had come here for. She could feel it.

Before dawn, pleased with her prize, Xerana returned to her wandering ship and began studying her treasure as she set off into the lonely darkness again.

Keeping to herself, for she had no companions, Xerana sat among all the artifacts she had collected. As she roamed the stars in her ship in search of answers, she had compiled a repository of xel'naga artifacts. She did not hoard these treasures or keep them merely as her personal possessions. They were for research, and each tiny item held one small part of the key to the understanding that the dark templar so desired.

Xerana spent hour upon hour meditating, trying to piece together what was known of the ancient lost race so that she could derive fresh insights. She had already spent nearly a century digging up answers in the cold Void and in the vibrant genes of her race. In a separate chamber, where she went when she allowed herself to feel lonely, Xerana also kept many mementos of her beloved planet, Aiur, which she would probably never see again.

As her ship cruised along, Xerana studied the worn, broken piece of the obelisk. After studying it almost to the point of putting herself into a trance, Xerana finally found a comparison among her other tiny specimens, and was able to decipher a set of runes. She translated a fragment, perhaps a bit of poetry or a legend that the xel'naga progenitors would have told each other as darkness gathered.

Maybe with this additional piece of data she could add to the history the dark templar already knew. She might use it to make a connection with other seemingly disparate artifacts.

She felt excitement and pride build within her, though she knew there were many secrets left to uncover. As her ship moved along, continuing its search, Xerana felt that a breakthrough was near, that the answers to her most important questions were so close she could almost touch them.

CHAPTER 5

UNDER THE COMMAND OF GENERAL EDMUND Duke, the warships of Alpha Squadron were always ready for battle. In fact, the troops were eager for it.

The devastating first conflict with the zerg and the protoss had obliterated the fringe colony worlds of Chau Sara and Mar Sara, the Confederacy government world of Tarsonis, and the protoss home planet of Aiur.

Duke hated aliens—of any flavor. He woke up at night in his flagship cabin trying to strangle the sweaty sheets on his bunk.

In the upheavals of the recent war, the charismatic rebel Arcturus Mengsk, leader of the violent Sons of Korhal, had seized command of what had been the Terran Confederacy and crowned himself the new emperor. Duke didn't think the man was particularly honorable or trustworthy or even talented. Mengsk was a politician, after all.

Different government, same military. General Duke just did his job.

Since he wanted to keep his command, Duke had no compunction about obeying whatever Emperor Arcturus Mengsk told him to do. The general knew who issued his orders.

Many of the vessels had been damaged in the conflict, including his flagship, the *Norad II*. Since then, however, the new Emperor Mengsk had spent a lot of money to pump up the military. Alpha Squadron's damaged ships had been refurbished, their weapons had been reloaded, and they had been sent out into space again.

His fleet consisted of battlecruisers, wraiths, science vessels, and dropships, a full-fledged force ready for a dangerous galaxy. The cursed protoss and zerg were still out there somewhere.

Alpha Squadron had left Korhal, the emperor's new capital planet, which had been damaged by Confederacy vengeance many years before. But Arcturus Mengsk had had the last laugh . . . and General Duke still had his military command. Nothing else mattered much to the general.

For months, the ships of Alpha Squadron had been out on routine survey missions, mapping potential colony worlds, reestablishing contact with others that had fallen by the wayside. Duke could not have imagined a more boring assignment—not for a brilliant strategist like himself, and not for his loyal soldiers either.

But the political situation with the newly formed Terran Dominion was still unsteady, and Mengsk had picked his own men to form the Imperial Guard close to home. Presumably, General Duke had not yet convinced the emperor of his loyalty, so he and Alpha Squadron were dispatched far away, where they could cause little trouble.

Duke preferred to avoid politics anyway, and if those two malicious species wanted to come back for another dogfight, he'd be happy to give it to them, all right. Damned aliens! In any case, the general expected to uncover more information and more strongholds of the evil zerg or the treacherous protoss—he didn't care which—out here in the uncharted areas than he would ever find back home in the civilized sectors.

After so much time on patrol, General Duke had assessed the fleet's resources, looked at their military capabilities, and given orders for Alpha Squadron to stop at the next vespene-rich asteroid field. He intended to stuff his ships to the gills with more resources than the emperor had allowed him. Now, he stood on the flagship, the rebuilt and completely repaired *Norad II*—now named *Norad III*—a battle-cruiser with all the punch General Duke could ever wish for.

Ready to go.

He just wished he had something to *fight* against, rather than doing this continuous . . . social studies homework assignment. Did Emperor Mengsk really want to know about the status of podunk colony worlds? Surely the new ruler of the Terran Dominion had more important things on his mind.

Duke looked out the portholes of his flagship and

watched the activity around him in space. All his soldiers moved efficiently—not because they were trying
to impress their commander, but because they were
truly that *good*. He had seen to that himself.

On vespene-rich asteroids in the belt, faint wisps of
the silvery gas escaped into space from the low gravity, making the floating rocks look like played-out
comets. Space Construction Vehicles, or SCVs, found
the most powerful geysers and set down, using
asteroid materials to build impromptu refineries,
which captured and distilled the gas into usable form.
The SCVs bustled about like honeybees in a field of
flowers, harvesting the gas and returning to the
fleet with clear barrels of the fuel.

Soon Duke's ships would be more than ready for
anything . . . and, again, with nothing important to do.

The task took no longer than necessary, following
standard operating procedures. Still Duke paced the
deck, glancing at status screens, barking orders to his
officers, prowling about looking for something useful
for his ships to do. Scouts in powered suits retrieved
other valuable minerals from the asteroids in order to
bring all of Alpha Squadron's ships and supplies up to
optimal levels.

During a lull, his helmsman and weapons officer,
Lieutenant Scott, chose to speak up. "General, sir,
might I ask you a question? Permission to speak
freely?" Tall, handsome, and forthright, Scott was well
respected by the other marines.

"I assume all my officers have brains in their heads,

Lieutenant. Otherwise, I'd just commission a crew of robots." Duke was bored enough to give the young man his permission, though normally such boldness would have earned him a reprimand.

"I assume you have a plan, sir?" Lieutenant Scott said. "Are we waiting to make our move?"

"I always have a plan," Duke said gruffly.

"What kind of plan, sir? Are we going to strike back at the unlawful Dominion and overthrow Emperor Mengsk? Are we going to help establish a government in exile for the overthrown Terran Confederacy?"

"Enough, Lieutenant!" General Duke said, raising his voice to a roar. "If the emperor hears such words he will convict you of treason."

"But, General, sir—they are *rebels*." Scott seemed dubious. "Sons of Korhal. They were our enemies."

Duke pounded his fist on the command console of the *Norad III*. "They are *currently* the lawful government of all terrans. Would you have me become a rebel myself, just so that I can wreak vengeance on another pack of rebels? May I remind you that our duty is to follow the orders of our commander in chief. After the destruction of Tarsonis, and now that we've finally driven back the zerg, our legal political leader just happens to be Emperor Mengsk. You would do well not to forget that, son."

Lieutenant Scott realized it was time to hold any further comments in check.

Duke lowered his voice, knowing that all of his marines were impatient to strike against the vile aliens. "We are engaged in a fight for the human race, Lieutenant. Let's keep our priorities where they belong."

The other officers on the bridge, many of whom probably felt the same as Lieutenant Scott, took the reprimand to heart and very quickly found urgent duties with which to occupy themselves.

The general sat back in his command chair, watching the remaining tedious operations taking place out in the asteroid belt. A military leader must always remain focused on his goal. He did not neglect attention to details. A conflict could be won or lost because of a tiny item that someone had overlooked.

Alpha Squadron had always prided itself on being the first military unit into a fight, and also the first group out. Right now, though, there was no place to go. Even when the mineral and vespene operations were completed in the asteroids and the ships withdrew to begin their slow journey through space again, General Duke knew that nothing exciting would happen.

He retired to his quarters after turning over command to a surprised Lieutenant Scott. He saw no tactical advantage to their current mission and decided to take some time to hone his skills.

General Duke spent the next three days at his own computer screens, challenging himself with exciting tactical war games in order to sharpen his edge. He played scenario after scenario, beating the computer every time.

Still, he was getting tired of nothing happening. He was, after all, a man of action.

CHAPTER 6

OCTAVIA AND LARS STOOD AT THE BASE OF THE steep, crumbled slope where great rocks and cascades of soil had broken away and tumbled down to expose the alien object.

Octavia leaned against the robo-harvester. Brownish gray dirt fell away from the side of the gigantic tractor. Running a hand through her brown curls, she continued to assess the ominous, pulsing construction from a distance. But Lars, as usual, bounded ahead, his eagerness and curiosity overwhelming his common sense.

Her brother had always wanted to be first, to run the fastest, to build the tallest structure, to reach the top of the hill before Octavia or their few other young settler companions could. Now Lars used hands and feet to clamber up the sharp, raw edges of rock that had fallen down during the previous night's storm and earthquake.

She followed him, her breath coming heavy in

the sour-smelling air. The freshly overturned dirt had an odd taint, as if it had spoiled long ago. The colonists knew from experience that only a few crops could survive in Bhekar Ro's soil. Octavia was used to the smell, of course, and rarely noticed it except after a hard rain. In filmbooks, she had seen lush agricultural worlds, verdant fields heavy with crops. She never knew whether to believe such fantasies.

Now she climbed after her brother, her hands and clothes growing dirty. Dirt was just another part of their harsh daily lives as farmers.

"Hey, look at this!" Lars called, and in a few moments she had clambered up closer to the smooth, curving walls of the bizarre structure.

Protruding from the newly exposed area were giant snowflake crystals, shards of transparent material that seethed with strange energy, each fragment longer than her arm. Octavia pressed one hand against the slick surface, finding it achingly cold, but not icy. A strange sensation like an electric tingle ran through the whorls of her palm and fingertips as if some energy were mapping her cellular structure and studying it.

"Now *these* are interesting," Lars said, his hazel eyes alive with wonder. "What do you think we could use them for? I bet we could take a full load of these crystals back on the robo-harvester."

"Why? To make giant necklaces for the old farmwives?" Octavia said, pulling her hand away from the crystalline formation. Her fingers continued to tingle.

Lars grinned his cocky grin. "I don't know about those farmwives, but I have a feeling Cyn McCarthy might like one."

Octavia raised her eyebrows. So, her independent brother had actually noticed that the pretty young widow was interested in him romantically. Far be it from Octavia to discourage him. Maybe he wasn't as dense as she had thought!

"All right, Lars, I admit the crystals *might* be useful. But before you start making grandiose plans, let's be practical, here—just for a few minutes, please? I suggest we look around. And be careful not to change anything until we understand more."

Lars grinned at her and climbed up the slope again toward the gleaming, labyrinthine structure. "Well, the way to find out more is to do some poking around. Let's split up and we can cover more ground."

"Splitting up is never a good idea," Octavia said, knowing the warning would be ignored by her enthusiastic brother.

"You be careful, and I'll be careful," he said, "and we'll be back in time to fix the seismographs by midday."

Octavia clamped her lips together and didn't bother to contradict him. She wasn't worried about the seismographs in the least.

The beautiful crystalline protrusions stuck out all around them at odd angles like the spines of a ruffled urchin lizard. Lars moved toward the eerie facade of the object itself, fascinated by the mysteries that drew him.

Octavia moved more slowly, pausing to study the crystals, trying to understand how they grew, where they came from. It seemed as if they had been planted around this buried object as . . . markers? Defenses? Some sort of message?

Puffing and sweating, though the effort did not diminish his exuberant grin, Lars reached the strange swirling shapes that formed the walls and openings of the giant object. The structural material was a pearlescent green, lit from within like some sort of hardened bioluminescent slime. He stood back, appraising the enormous structure. From his furrowed brow and quickly moving eyes, Octavia could tell that her brother wasn't trying to understand the artifact, but was merely trying to choose the best means of getting inside.

Lars touched the exposed material. All of the soil and dust had flaked off, as if the object had a kind of static charge that repelled grime and dirt. He rapped against the wall with his knuckles, then held up his hand. "It sort of tingles. I can't tell if the material is plastic or glass or some kind of organic extrusion. Interesting."

"You promised to be careful," she called. "And I've got a bad feeling about this."

He looked down at her with raised eyebrows. "You always have bad feelings, Octavia."

Her brother dismissed her concerns, but then Lars

had never been as sensitive as she was. Octavia often had a knack for foreseeing events, for feeling when to avoid a certain situation. She had no hard proof, of course, but she was confident that her premonitions were correct. "And when have I ever been wrong, Lars?"

He didn't answer.

She knelt by one of the largest crystals and touched it again, running her hands over the slick surface. The odd cold tingle of energy called out to her, trying to communicate something that she couldn't comprehend. Overall, around this entire structure, Octavia felt a brooding, sleeping presence, something indescribable, buried and not yet awakened.

A frisson of inexplicable energy touched her mind, but she didn't know how to pursue the feeling, to explore it. It was an odd probing sensation, but whatever produced the feeling clearly didn't understand her or recognize her humanity.

Octavia swallowed hard in a dry throat and withdrew from the powerful crystal. The connection in her mind faded, but did not go entirely away.

Lars happily continued his explorations, poking his head into the smaller openings and then finally walking into a large, curving orifice that led deeper into the structure.

Octavia moved slowly, reaching the top and looking into the dark, cool opening where her brother had disappeared. Odd odors wafted from inside, like a rich mulch, something sizzling and alive. Though the power contained within the artifact intimidated her, she didn't feel that it was particularly evil or threatening. Just . . . unlike anything she had ever encountered before.

His voice called back to her, echoing yet damped by the solid walls of the structure. "Octavia, come in here! You won't believe the amazing things."

She stepped forward, peering into the shadows. She heard footsteps as he came hurrying back toward her. His eyes were aglow. "These passages are studded with more crystals and other strange objects, treasures, resources! We could use a pickax or a laser cutter to chop them out of the walls."

"You don't even know what they are, Lars," she said.

"I'll bet they'll bring a lot of credits once we sell them."

She didn't enter the artifact, but instead put her dirty hands on her hips. "Who would you sell them to, Lars? For what? Crops? Equipment? Nobody in Free Haven has anything to spare. And our colony hasn't traded with anybody since before you and I were born."

Grinning, Lars lowered his voice as if afraid someone might be eavesdropping. "This goes far beyond what Bhekar Ro can handle, Octavia. I think as soon as we get back, we need to contact the terran government. We'll be rich! Imagine what we can sell this for. Even you have to admit that this is interesting—the find of a lifetime. Our colony can acquire new equipment, new seed stock, maybe even new workers to bolster our population. We've lost so many families in the past few years."

Octavia felt her heart sink as she remembered their dead parents and all the specialists and just plain good people who had died in the spore plagues or in natural disasters or in any number of other tragedies that had beset Bhekar Ro since its formation. She felt her brother's optimism and imagined all the wonders he had described, realizing that—for once—Lars might actually be right in his ambitions.

Then she made a disbelieving sound. Even if this artifact turned out to be something truly remarkable, meeting all of the hopeful criteria Lars envisioned, the colony's communication link with the Terran Confederacy had been left unused for thirty-five of the forty years Free Haven had existed as a human settlement. The colonists had come here to get away from terran governments, to live for themselves and be self-sufficient. Their parents and grandparents had hated any interference or oppression, and few of the colonists would choose to call attention to themselves again.

"I don't think the others would agree, especially not Mayor Nik," Octavia said. "I'm not convinced that even something like this is worth bringing the Confederacy back to breathe down our necks. You've heard the stories Grandfather used to tell. It could damage our way of life."

Now Lars looked at her in astonishment. "Our *way of life*? Could it get any worse? Do the list of pros and cons for yourself, and you'll be convinced." He turned around and quickly moved deeper into the glowing corridors.

Octavia followed him, still sensing the oppressive mental presence around her, feeling it grow more powerful. Lars hurried farther along, stopping to rap against walls with his fist, listening to the echo, trying to discover differences.

Striations of color ran through the walls like veins of ore . . . or maybe like the blood vessels of an alien creature. He sniffed, then studied the wall carefully. He tried to scratch it with his fingernails, but could make no mark. He shook his head and moved on.

Lars had always dreamed of being a prospector, an archaeologist, an explorer here on this largely unmapped world. But nobody on Bhekar Ro had much chance to be more than a simple farmer, working through every hour of gloomy daylight just to keep the colony functioning. Octavia didn't have the heart to drain away her brother's enjoyment right now. He had been waiting for an opportunity like this all his life.

Octavia felt a sudden reluctance to go deeper into the chambers of the artifact, as if the air were thickening around her. The odd psychic energy formed a wall, slowly pushing her back.

Lars didn't seem to feel it at all. He turned to examine an arch in the tunnel where it hooked to the left, and saw a cluster of beehive-shaped objects made of something smooth and translucent. They looked almost like large, faceted jewels that grew out of the walls.

"Come on!" Standing in the arched opening of the side tunnel, Lars reached up with one hand to the cluster. As soon as he grasped one of the brightly colored protrusions, though, the entire light and atmosphere in the artifact changed slightly. It was as if he had triggered something.

His hand remained fastened to the nodule. His face fell, and an instant later, he froze. Octavia sensed a crackle of energy flowing through him. All of the crystal shards protruding from the walls and those outside the artifact glowed brighter, as if they had been switched on.

"Lars!" she shouted.

But he couldn't move, couldn't even make a sound.

Sizzling beams shot out like lightning bolts, linking one crystal after another in a webwork. Bright light ricocheted down the corridors, blinding Octavia. She tried to move, but it all happened so fast.

Lars stood within the arched opening like an insect trapped on a microscope slide, and the brilliant beams from the crystals flooded over him like spotlights, scanning him, crashing into his body. In a flash, his skin turned completely white. His bones and his muscles glowed from inside, as if he had become a luminous substance through and through, every cell converted to pure energy.

Then the walls themselves took on the same blinding white glow, as if they were absorbing Lars down to the last atom. Suddenly the lightning stopped. All the lights faded to their former eerie dimness.

And Lars was gone. Not even a shadow remained.

Two of the large crystals outside the artifact shattered, and sparks flickered down the corridors, bursting other crystals in a chain reaction, as if Lars had been something unpalatable, a substance this artifact could not digest.

Smoke curled through the tunnels. The deafening sounds quieted, leaving only the faint echo of a scream. Octavia couldn't tell if it was the last sound made by her brother or her own wordless cry.

After a lull of less than a second, the walls brightened again, the larger crystals shimmering. Lightning bolts crackled. Lars had awakened something ominous, and Octavia wondered if his death might bring about the destruction of them all.

Octavia turned and scrambled down the smooth tunnel to the opening. Toward daylight. She ran faster, terror making her eyes wide, her mind numb. Too many things were happening. She wanted to go back and search for her brother, to see if anything of his body remained.

But her drive for self-preservation kicked in. She knew the artifact wasn't done yet.

Octavia bounded out of the opening and down the boulder-strewn slope, somehow keeping her feet under her, dropping from one rock to another, steadying herself with her hands and spreading her arms to keep her balance.

The hillside vibrated harder. Now all the large crystals that had seemed so beautiful a moment ago looked like loaded weapons, tapping energy reservoirs that summoned lightning from within their atomic structure.

Her retreat was a blur. Somehow, faster than she had ever imagined she could move, Octavia found herself back at the robo-harvester, leaning against the mud-encrusted treads. Behind her, on the steep hillside, the tall crystals ignited. Lightning bolts that sparkled like blue spiderwebs connected them all, drawing their power together and weaving it into a knot of energy until all the stray threads converged.

Finally, a beacon of sound and light—some sort of giant transmission—speared upward into the sky and far out into space. It was not directed at her at all, but somewhere distant. To something *not human.*

The shock wave knocked Octavia flat, sending her sprawling on the broken ground. She could barely hold on as the pulsing signal rippled and tore through the air.

Out of breath, frantic, she crawled up the treads of the robo-harvester. As she grabbed the door of the armored cab, her head throbbed and her ears rang. She threw herself inside, slammed the door, and collapsed on the seat. She could barely hear anything.

For the moment she felt protected, but not enough. Moving blindly, she started the engine of the enormous vehicle, wheeled it around on its treads, and crunched over the broken ground at top speed, sending rocks and dirt clods flying as she raced across the valley. She had to get back to Free Haven.

Octavia couldn't think straight, could not yet address in her mind what had happened to her brother, what she had seen with her own eyes.

But she knew she had to warn the other colonists.

CHAPTER 7

OUT IN DEEP SPACE, SURROUNDED BY THE MOST powerful warships of the protoss expeditionary force, Executor Koronis sought the privacy and refuge of his own quarters aboard the flagship carrier *Qel'Ha*. There he could contemplate his mission, his destiny, and the fate of his race.

He could sense through his nerve appendages all of the loyal protoss who served aboard the ships in his fleet: the industrialists, scientists, and workers in the Khalai class; the ferociously dedicated zealots and other soldiers in the determined warrior class, called the templar. He even sensed the stern governmental-religious caste of judicators, who oversaw the prosecution of this mission and maintained focus on the Khala.

But as he tried to find peace and contemplation, Koronis could feel the utter misery and failure of his entire crew. The Executor's shoulders slumped, causing the stiff pointed pads of his uniform to sag. Aiur had suffered a devastating attack by the zerg and had very nearly been destroyed, but Koronis's expeditionary force had been far from the scene of carnage, far from their families and homes. They had not helped at all. They had failed. And the entire protoss race had teetered on the brink of extinction.

It was a difficult burden to bear.

Koronis sat in his polished curved meditation seat and held in his scaly hands a small fragment of a worn but still glittering crystal. The gem merchant had told him that the ancient prophet Khas had used this shard when he discovered the telepathic Way of the Khala. The Khala had finally unified the protoss, brought them together through their mental abilities, and ended the Aeon of Strife that had torn their civilization apart for so long.

Koronis did not know if the myth surrounding the origin of this Khaydarin crystal was true or merely a story concocted by a trader wishing to get a better price, but the executor took comfort from the possibility. He stared into the crystal, concentrating his mental energies. His depthless golden eyes burned like small suns, looking deep within the crystal structure, far into the corners of the universe. His textured gray face rippled as he concentrated, brow ridges furrowing, ornamented shoulders hunched. His mouthless chin remained firm.

Many decades ago the Protoss Conclave had sent out Koronis and his expeditionary force on a long-term mission far beyond the fringes of the Koprulu

Sector. Since the protoss were a long-lived race, they did not worry about decades or even centuries, and he had been proud to be chosen. Before departing, Koronis had been named executor, a high rank held by very few, for his mission had been considered extremely important.

He and his crew had been dispatched to search for any sign of the heretical dark templar, who had refused to join the Khala and kept themselves separate from the unified mental presence of the protoss. The judicators in the Conclave could not accept such a blight on protoss society. They commanded that the dark templar must be either brought into the fold or destroyed. Koronis had never considered the dark templar to be a great threat and would have preferred to leave the exiles alone, but the fanatical Conclave politicians made such decisions, not he.

Koronis was far more interested in the second part of his mission: to search for any remnants of the ancient progenitor race, the Xel'Naga, who had created the protoss as their special children, their First Born.

Recent discoveries proved that the xel'naga had created the hostile zerg as well, perhaps intending the zerg to supplant the First Born. Executor Koronis did not know what to think of that, but it seemed to bespeak the continued failure and disappointment of his people.

As he contemplated, the Khaydarin crystal began to glow with a warm humming. At first Koronis took strength from it, until the power of the crystal artifact also amplified his ability to sense the anguish and despair that ran rampant through his crew.

He closed his gleaming eyes and withdrew his mind from the Khaydarin crystal. So far, after decades of searching, the *Qel'Ha* had uncovered no evidence of the Xel'Naga. Nor had they found any of the dark templar.

His expeditionary force was a mighty fleet that could have made a difference in the defense of Aiur against the zerg; instead, for years they had wasted their time out here on the fringes of inhabited space. Koronis had nothing to show for it. With his three-fingered hand he held the long, colorful sash that designated his rank and office, a proud symbol that now seemed meaningless to him.

The shield door at the entry to his quarters slid upward, and the imposing figure of Judicator Amdor stood in the corridor, his red-orange eyes blazing. A deep purple robe was draped around him, flowing as if in reflection of his moods or mental energies. Jeweled shoulder pads and metal-scaled headgear made Amdor look ominous and impressive. On purpose.

As a powerful political representative of the Conclave, Judicator Amdor did not feel the need to show Koronis courtesy. There would have been some friction between the two of them if the commander had allowed it, but he was loyal to his race and to his mission and did not rise to the occasional criticisms that the stern judicator heaped upon him. Amdor seemed to think the expedition's failure was the Executor's fault.

With no lips to move, no mouths to form words, all protoss communicated through tight, telepathic bursts. The judicator focused his conversation closely enough that no eavesdroppers could pick up even a hint of his sentences, though at times the mental spike was so sharp that it caused Koronis a faint twinge of pain. He showed none of it, however, simply turned and listened to what the judicator had to say.

"This disgrace has gone on long enough, Executor. Our expeditionary force must return to Aiur. We are too late to help with the great battle against the zerg, but we can assist with rebuilding. Turn the *Qel'Ha* around, and we will voyage back home. We must salvage what we can."

The zerg Overmind had been obliterated, and Aiur was saved, though at the cost of devastating much of the land. Tassadar, the accused traitor, had combined the powers of the Khala with secrets learned from the Void. Judicator Amdor called Tassadar's actions a despicable heresy taught him by the dark templar, but Koronis could not fault the hero for his results.

He wished he had been there to see the end. It would have been a marvelous sight . . .

Without hurrying, the executor put away his crystal fragment and rose from his meditation chair. He straightened his sash and adjusted his extravagantly pointed shoulder pads.

Koronis's mental control was not as precise as that of the Judicator's, and Amdor caught some flicker of his musings. "Tassadar was no hero!" he said, his thought-words sharp. "He sacrificed his dedication to the Khala in order to achieve glory for himself and short-term gain."

Surprised, the executor faced Amdor in the ship's corridor outside of his quarters. "But he saved the protoss and sacrificed himself in the process. I hardly believe you can ascribe selfish motives to what Tassadar achieved."

"The greatest thing he achieved," Amdor snapped in return, "was that by eradicating the zerg and devastating Aiur, he cleansed the protoss race! In the aftermath of this disaster, we now have the opportunity to rebuild, to burn out the cancerous heretics that have corrupted our dedication to the Khala. I am eager to return home so that I can help the Conclave to ensure that we do not slip down this dark and ill-advised path."

Seeing no point in arguing, Koronis acquiesced. He, too, wanted to return home, even without Amdor's insistence. "I exist to serve the Khala."

When the two of them reached the bridge, the executor took over the *Qel'Ha*'s egg-shaped command chair. Judicator Amdor stood beside him like a grim parent, as if not convinced the commander would do as he had promised.

With the psychic booster, Koronis sent a message to all the protoss minds in his fleet. "We will go home. We have work to do with our families and our cities and our world. Since we could not help when Aiur needed us most, we must be willing to give our lives and our minds to assist now . . . to make up for not being there."

Through the mental link of his nerve appendages, Koronis felt a surge of relief and enthusiasm ripple through the crew, a hope that raised them above their gloom. The engines of the fleet's carriers and flanking ships powered up. The navigators calculated a course that would take them back to the heart of protoss space.

But before they could embark, the psychic communication loops—broad spiderweb transceivers woven into the hulls of the ships—received a powerful message pulse. A distant, alien signal.

The eerie notes vibrated through Koronis's mind, through the ships, through the entire crew. A cry, a shout, an indecipherable message.

The throbbing signal continued to pound, grating on the Executor's nerves, haunting yet somehow familiar. Judicator Amdor stood stiffly, confused at first, then startled.

When the distant call finally stopped, all the protoss remained stunned. The executor directed his thought-speech to Amdor, although others in the vicinity caught the fringes of his excited thoughts. "There is something of the xel'naga in that signal! I recognize the symbols and the tones. Do you not hear it? The message is . . . urgent."

"And quite powerful," Amdor said. "But what xel'naga device could broadcast a signal so strong and clear as to reach this far?" The judicator turned his sharp gaze to the technical Khalai working at the communications equipment on the *Qel'Ha*'s bridge.

One of the officers sent a quick mental burst. "We have tracked the signal back to a small planet. Uninhabited, as far as we know."

Koronis studied the coordinates, quickly calculated how long it would take the expeditionary force to go there. He sent his thought clearly to Amdor. "Judicator, this signal offers us the opportunity to return to Aiur with some measure of honor and success—not as complete failures. If we can indeed find an important xel'naga device, we will accomplish our mission of discovery and return to Aiur as heroes. We can bring hope to our people."

The judicator nodded. "If the signal came from the Wanderers from Afar, it may well be an omen. We are the First Born, and our destiny is to retrieve our race's lost glory. Finding whatever sent this signal could be a huge step toward achieving that goal."

"En taro Adun," Koronis said, using the honor salute that meant "in honor of Adun," a great protoss hero.

"En taro Adun," the judicator responded curtly, as if distracted and already making plans.

Feeling confident for the first time since he had received the terrible news about Aiur, Executor Koronis summoned a robotic observer and commanded that it be dispatched immediately to the source of the mysterious xel'naga signal.

CHAPTER 8

GONE. LARS WAS GONE.

The thought beat at Octavia's mind in rhythm with the thumping treads of the robo-harvester as she careened across the long, rugged kilometers toward the settlement. Her hands and feet operated the heavy equipment without any help from her conscious mind, for she had room for only one thought there: *Lars is dead!* She could hardly wrap her mind around it.

The robo-harvester lurched and bounced, crashing over dirt piles and mounds of rock debris. The rocking motion twisted her neck and shoulders, but she gritted her teeth.

Overhead, the same glider hawk still rested on high breezes, scanning the ground in a fruitless search for food . . .

The massive vehicle ground its way up the steep slope, back and forth against the grade as boulders and loose dirt sprayed beneath the flurry of treads.

Octavia's view of the stark landscape in front of her dimmed and grew blurry, as if a fog had rolled into the broad valley. She tried to clear the windshield but soon realized that the problem was with her own eyes.

Octavia was not given to bouts of weeping, and she didn't have time for it now. She had to get back to Free Haven to sound the alarm. To tell the other settlers about the ominous, murderous artifact that had been uncovered by the storm. She had always been far too practical to waste time on useless displays of emotion—not because she didn't care when a friend or family member died. It was a survival mechanism. Those colonists who allowed themselves to become easily depressed by the cruel vagaries of life here soon became listless, careless. And carelessness on Bhekar Ro usually meant a speedy death.

As far as Octavia could recall, she had cried only a few times before: once after the death of her grandparents, another time about a week after her parents' deaths from the spore blight, during the next thunderous storm when the realization had hit her like a slap in the face that her father would never be there to comfort her again. Tears were such an unaccustomed sensation that she hardly recognized it. *Lars is gone!*

But then, as salty drops flowed down her cheeks, her anger began to flow as well. What a ridiculous waste! It didn't make any sense. And what *was* that thing out there on the ridge? It obviously wasn't of terran origin.

Why had she allowed Lars to talk her into going out there? What had they stood to gain from it? Yet Lars, with his insatiable curiosity, had felt the need to go. He had only been exploring.

And the thing had murdered her brother. *Murdered.* Stolen Lars from her forever—and for what? Who could say?

One thing she did know, however. She had to warn the other colonists before the artifact could claim any more lives.

The village meeting hall was filled to overflowing with nearly two thousand grumbling settlers. Octavia could hear snatches of conversation from around the hall.

"What kind of emergency? Wasn't the storm emergency enough?"

"I have crops to replant. Couldn't this wait?"

"I heard Lars Bren found something."

"*I* heard he's disappeared!"

" . . . better hurry it up or I'll be leaving."

At last, Mayor "Nik" Nikolai took his place on the low platform at the front of the room and called the meeting to order. He was a distractible and not overly charismatic person under normal circumstances, but at the age of twenty-eight he was already considered an established, respected administrator, more or less. He banged on his podium, trying to get the audience to settle down.

"Excuse me! Hello? Octavia Bren has some serious news for us." He paused a moment, looking around. "Serious enough that I thought we might need to take a vote about what to do after you hear what she has to say."

"Can't you just sum it up and we'll take a vote and get out of here?" Shayna Bradshaw yelled from the audience. "My irrigation system is clogged again, and—"

The mayor shook his head. "I think it'll be best if I let Octavia tell you in her own words."

Octavia gritted her teeth at the grumbling in the room and stepped onto the platform. She clung to her anger instead of her grief. How hardened they had all become to news of tragedy or calamity. Somehow she had to make them understand how important this was. She cleared her throat and put as much volume and authority into her seventeen-year-old voice as she could. "I know most of you believe there's nothing important enough, nothing *urgent* enough to justify calling all of you here. Shocks and disappointments, even death, have become part of our everyday life."

"So get to the point!" old Rastin called from the center of the room.

"Where's your brother?" called Cyn McCarthy, looking hopeful.

Octavia drew a deep steadying breath and started again. "Lars is dead." She held up a hand to forestall the automatic murmurs of sympathy from the gathered crowd. "He was killed by something out on a ridge about twelve klicks from here. An alien artifact that was buried inside the mountain. Something huge."

"Did you say alien?" Mayor Nikolai was surprised.

"Yes, *alien!* We are not alone here on Bhekar Ro!"

Octavia described what had happened. Haltingly, she told about their exploration of the artifact, and when she got to the part with the bright beams of light spearing across her brother's body, flashing around him as he disintegrated, her throat seized up and refused to work. She felt a hand on her arm and looked up to see Cyn McCarthy standing next to her, a stricken look on the young widow's freckled face.

"Seems to me the answer's simple," old Rastin said dismissively. "Nobody in the colony goes near that thing again. Leave it alone. If we expand, we just go th' other direction."

Octavia gritted her teeth again, and anger gave her back her voice. Unless she convinced the settlers that this was serious, they might all die.

"Ignoring it isn't good enough. Something else happened out there. As I was leaving that *thing*, it sent a signal up into space. Some kind of transmission, or alarm, or homing beacon. The light was so bright it almost blinded me, and the sound shook the ground and threw me off my feet."

"Hey, was that right before noon for about two minutes?" asked Kiernan Warner from the front row.

"I think I heard that! If it was twelve klicks away, it must've been really loud."

"Do you think the artifact was trying to communicate with us?" Lyn's younger brother Wes asked in an alarmed tone.

Octavia shook her head. "The beacon went straight up into space, as if it thought someone was out there waiting to get its signal. It might have been trying to communicate with someone, but definitely not *us.*"

The room erupted with exclamations, questions, and suggestions, and Octavia knew she had gotten their attention.

Mayor Nikolai took the stage again and held up his hands for quiet. When the room settled down slightly, he said, "Octavia believes we should contact the Terran Confederacy. Let them know what we've found here."

A few of the colonists began to voice objections, but were quickly shushed by their neighbors.

"We don't know if that was a comm beacon or not, but if more of those things show up on Bhekar Ro, we may not be able to handle the situation ourselves," Mayor Nikolai said.

"This is our planet!" Wes's cousin Jon said.

Octavia spoke up again. "Even if the artifact is the only one of its kind, we don't know what it can do. Now that it's been unearthed, it might become aggressive and go after our settlement. It might even cause earthquakes that could wipe us all out."

"Put it to a vote," Jon yelled.

"Yeah, we've heard enough," Kiernan added.

"My irrigation system is still leaking," Shayna Bradshaw grumbled.

To Octavia's relief, with the exception of three colonists, the vote was unanimous. A message would be sent to the last-known terran government. Maybe the Confederacy had experience with such matters.

Octavia paced anxiously outside the communications turret that stood at an intersection across from the plaza at the center of the village. The comm system was like the antique missile turret at the center of the plaza in that no one knew if the equipment still worked. It had not been used for long-range communication in dozens of years, only for contacting outlying farms and settlements during emergency situations.

The mayor had insisted on complete privacy inside the turret while making the transmission attempt. He had been shut inside the tower for forty-five minutes now. Octavia hoped that was a good sign. Or maybe he couldn't figure out how to operate the transmitter.

Finally, Mayor Nikolai emerged wearing a bemused expression. He ran a hand through his spiky blond hair, looking very satisfied with himself.

"Did you get through?" Octavia asked. "Did you talk to the Terran Confederacy?"

"Well, not exactly. It seems the Confederacy fell apart and now the government is called the Terran Dominion.

The guy I talked to called himself the emperor—pretty impressive, I suppose. Name of Arcturus Mengsk. He seemed interested in what we found, asked a lot of questions. Told me they'll probably send a military force out to investigate immediately."

Octavia heaved a sigh of relief. "Good. Then help is on the way."

Their troubles were over.

CHAPTER 9

AS HE LOUNGED BACK ON THE THRONE, NEWLY installed in the restored capital of Korhal, Emperor Arcturus Mengsk felt vindicated for all the years he had spent in guerrilla activities, scheming against the repressive Terran Confederacy.

The throne felt *right* to him, as if he had always deserved it. And he felt powerful.

In the background, a holoprojection was playing, repeating the magnificent speech he had given to all human beings on the event of his self-coronation. Mengsk never got tired of hearing the words.

"Fellow terrans, I come to you, in the wake of recent events, to issue a call to reason. Let no human deny the perils of our time. While we battle one another, divided by the petty strife of our common history, the tide of a greater conflict is turning against us, threatening to destroy all that we have accomplished."

Very dramatic. Very compelling. Mengsk had practiced the speech many times in front of numerous advisors.

It had been months now since the overthrow of the Terran Confederacy, when Mengsk himself had arranged to lure the evil zerg minions to the capital planet of Tarsonis. There, the voracious aliens had done Mengsk's destructive work for him. And better still, he had managed to make it appear that he was the hope of all humans, a knight in shining armor.

His image continued to speak. "It is time for us as nations and as individuals to set aside our long-standing feuds and unite. The tides of an unwinnable war are upon us, and we must seek refuge upon higher ground lest we be swept away by the flood.

"With our enemies left unchecked, who will you turn to for protection?"

Good words, he thought, *a nice slogan.* Worth repeating.

Much remained to be done, though. Emperor Mengsk had worlds to subdue, governments to reestablish, figureheads to put into place.

And now he had received this odd message from the forgotten colony of Bhekar Ro.

Mengsk shifted in his throne, looking at a transcript of the communiqué. He wanted to review every word of his conversation with the colony's mayor, Jacob Nikolai. *Never heard of him before.*

Running his well-manicured fingers down his bushy whiskers, Mengsk frowned, wondering what to do about the situation. His initial instinct had been to ignore the request for assistance. Bhekar Ro was not on the list of important worlds on which the new emperor needed to secure his grasp. Even the Confederacy had left them alone. Why should he really be concerned about a bunch of dirt farmers from a backwater world nobody had ever noticed?

Distracting sounds drifted to him from the rooms surrounding the throne chamber: loud hammering, buzzing diamond cutters, and sparking laser welders. Now that he had control of the terran government, Mengsk had ordered construction on a vast scale to begin on the devastated worlds, such as the restoration here on Korhal, which remained scarred from previous Confederate atrocities.

Over the din, his holo speech continued. "The devastation wrought by the alien invaders is self-evident. We have seen our homes and communities destroyed by the calculated blows of the protoss, we have seen firsthand our friends and loved ones consumed by the nightmarish zerg. Unprecedented and unimaginable though they may be, these are the signs of our time."

Infrastructure damaged by the zerg invasion and the protoss strikes on Mar Sara and Chau Sara needed to be healed and rebuilt—but those unimportant places could come later. First the emperor had to figure out how to squeeze more taxes from the populace so that he could restock his imperial treasury. Any planet that did not cheer Mengsk's presence loudly enough would find it far more difficult to receive funding and civil engineers for their construction projects.

"The time has come, my fellow terrans, to rally to a new banner. In unity lies strength. Already many of the dissident factions have joined us. Out of the many we shall forge an indivisible whole, under the authority of a single throne. And from that throne I shall watch over you."

He decided to make sure that this coronation speech was taught to all young students in the new Dominion. Revising history could well become a full-time job . . .

Mengsk poured himself a glass of rich purple klavva wine, drank it down quickly, then poured a second glass that he could savor. The decision about the strange alien object on Bhekar Ro rested squarely on his shoulders. He couldn't pass it off to anyone else—that was the *dis*advantage of being emperor. But Arcturus Mengsk had earned the right, earned this position, and he chided himself for complaining about the minor duties of a great ruler.

What exactly had those backwater settlers found? He had agreed to send assistance, but was it really worth his while to investigate?

One of his uniformed aides marched briskly into the opulent throne room and gave him a smart raised-fist salute that had been used by the Sons of Korhal. If Emperor Mengsk had his way, the salute would soon be accepted throughout the Terran Dominion.

The aide handed him a rolled document, which

Mengsk opened and studied. Ah, the daily list of scheduled executions! The emperor ran his fingernail down the numerous names and recognized few of them. He didn't remember what their crimes were, and right now he didn't have the time to check up on everything. Too many annoying details. Most of them must have been political prisoners or mutineers who refused to give up the old reins of the Terran Confederacy.

He began to check the cases one by one, but then decided he had more pressing matters to attend to. Mengsk simply stamped the entire list "Approved" and handed it back to the aide, who raised his fist in the Dominion salute again and hurried off to present the duly signed document to the Executioners Guild.

Another job done for the day.

His holo speech wound toward its conclusion. "From this day forward let no human make war upon any other human. Let no terran agency conspire against this New Beginning. And let no man consort with alien powers. And to all the enemies of human- ity: Seek not to bar our way. For we shall win through, no matter the cost."

Mengsk stared again at the summary of the conver- sation he'd had with Mayor Nikolai. *What to do?* he mused. There was no point in being suspicious that these settlers were lying to him or overblowing their discovery, since they were so far out of galactic politics that they hadn't known who Emperor Mengsk was, had not even *heard* of the Terran Dominion.

Still, who really cared if some clodhoppers dug up a big shiny rock and didn't know what to make of it?

Unless the thing had some value to it. Emperor Mengsk never reacted too spontaneously. What if this alien "thing" was actually something important, something he shouldn't ignore? It could be a new threat, something sinister left by the zerg or the protoss, strange races that still brought fear to his heart, even though he had used them to his own ends in order to crush his former rivals.

Did he dare dismiss this discovery without investigating it? What if the pulsing artifact were a powerful repository of knowledge? What if it contained valuable resources . . . or even a weapon? Alien artifacts were exceedingly rare. Emperor Arcturus Mengsk knew he needed all the help he could get while he cemented his hold on power.

He went into his war room and called up the glowing three-dimensional star maps that showed the Koprulu Sector. He glanced at the familiar stars and planetary systems, then had the computer add a tiny dot to mark the Bhekar Ro colony, using coordinates backtracked from the communications signal. The colonists had been quiet for so long that they had fallen off regular Confederacy records. Mengsk muttered at the incompetence of his predecessors.

He studied the surrounding area, then called up a tactical display that showed where all of his ships in the sector were currently stationed. With a smile on his bearded face he decided to dispatch General

Edmund Duke and his Alpha Squadron to investigate. They needed something to do anyway.

The gruff general, who was already in the vicinity, was expendable at this point. The mission would keep the man and his marines occupied, and Mengsk doubted the colonists would complain overmuch to the hard-as-nails officer. The emperor didn't mind giving General Duke a more interesting assignment— as long as it kept him safely away from Korhal for the time being.

Though Duke had taken an oath to the new Dominion, he had fought on the side of the Confederacy for many years. Mengsk remained uneasy about having such a forceful military leader with so much firepower at his disposal just sitting around and getting bored.

The general was a hardened military leader who had sworn to defend his new government—and such men did not take oaths lightly. Still, he didn't distrust the commander entirely. The emperor decided to give Duke and Alpha Squadron a chance to prove themselves.

The holoprojector reset itself and began to play the coronation speech again. "Fellow terrans, I come to you, in the wake of recent events, to issue a call to reason . . ."

He considered shutting it off, but decided to listen just one more time.

Mengsk wrote out orders and transmitted them to the communications facility, dispatching Alpha Squadron with all due haste to Bhekar Ro.

CHAPTER 10

AT DAWN OVER THE GREASY GRAY SKIES OF Bhekar Ro, thin clouds swirled and then rippled like a tainted oil stain atop stagnant water. The wastelands were quiet . . . too quiet.

With a crack of thunder in the dry air, the fabric of space tore and a warp-rift opened. A glider hawk reeled about, disrupted in its endless search for food.

As the echoes of the boom rippled across the valley, startling small rodents that eked out an existence among the hardy scrub brush, a protoss observer from the *Qel'Ha* appeared and hovered high in the sky. Observers were reconnaissance vessels sent out to gather information, but not to participate in actual combat.

Automatically following its programming, the observer switched on a micro-cloaking field and vanished from view. The drone craft descended, activating the complex sensor array that drained most of its operational energy, leaving nothing for system defenses.

Three-fold wing shields opened, guiding the single, cyclopean eye.

Then it began to search.

The observer proceeded across the uninhabited areas of Bhekar Ro, unchallenged and unnoticed. While flying headlong across the vast distance of space, it had not been able to pinpoint its coordinates precisely. But now, as the observer homed in on the location of the artifact's transmitted signal, it planted navigational beacons so that the *Qel'Ha* and the rest of the protoss expeditionary force could arrive precisely on target.

The observer spent hours circling overhead, approaching the broken mountainside where the half-uncovered organic oddity lay exposed in the morning light. Sending regular real-time reports back to Executor Koronis, the reconnaissance drone imaged and analyzed the artifact protruding from the mountainside. After its initial transmission, the object had lain quiet. Waiting.

Once the small drone had inspected every angle and approached as closely as its programming allowed without risk of disturbing the artifact that had sent the signal, it proceeded to make a wider reconnaissance. In compiling its overall tactical survey, the drone acquired images of the mountain ranges and detected—with no hint of surprise in its robotic mind—cultivated fields and outlying settlements of prefabricated buildings.

Assessing the situation, the observer closed in, still

cloaked, until it hovered over the central colony town on Bhekar Ro. It began to collect data on the human settlers, the resident population, and their defenses . . .

It was a morning like any other morning, but Octavia Bren had to face the day without her brother Lars.

The other colonists left her alone, even Mayor Nikolai, who was better known for talk than for practical action. She sat in the octagonal town square remembering Lars and their time together, how they had often discussed which unmarried colonists they each might consider as a mate, how hard they had worked, what they had hoped to accomplish, how the two had teased each other as young children . . .

It had been long enough now that the scars of her parents' deaths had healed. The other colonists were so familiar with unexpected tragedy that they sympathized with Octavia, but were not paralyzed with grief. Free Haven had suffered enough before, and would continue to endure the pain. It was their lot in life. But Octavia's grandparents had been convinced that this was a better existence than living under the Terran Confederacy. Here they were free—though at the moment Octavia could not be entirely sure that she preferred the constant uncertainty and brevity of life on Bhekar Ro.

Octavia wished she and her brother had never gone out to inspect the seismographs and automated mining stations, but Lars had been so excited about the discovery. She wished he could have been like the other colonists, never curious, never striving for more, just holding on to life as long as he could manage.

But then he wouldn't have been Lars.

As the morning brightened, Octavia stayed near the ornamental old missile turret, constructed there over an abandoned bunker by the first colonists. It was meant to be a sentry station, an automated defense that would watch the skies and protect Bhekar Ro—though from what, she didn't know. The missile turret had sat there silently for more than forty years. Nobody even believed it worked anymore.

Now, instead of being seen as a defense, the turret served as a reminder and a monument to what they had left behind in the Confederacy. Occasionally some colonists proposed dismantling it for parts, power cells, and materials, but the mayor had never gotten enough ambition to gather a crew.

Now, as Octavia sat there alone, thinking of her brother and staring up into the unpleasant, featureless sky, the missile turret suddenly clicked, hummed, and moved. System lights winked on, sputtered, then glowed bright.

She leaped to her feet and scrambled away with a shout. A few colonists came out of their homes to look at her, then saw the activation lights on the clunky metal structure and saw the turret move.

Its hydraulics hummed as components opened, rattled, and locked into place. A brilliant light shone from its top as the turret's tracking scanner swiveled. The automatic sensors centered in and targeted something invisible in the sky. Missile turrets were designed to automatically target and fire on incoming enemy aircraft, but they also served as sentry stations; their powerful sensors could detect even cloaked vessels.

This turret had not stirred in decades, but now it locked on, selected a missile, and loaded it into the launch rack, its mechanisms clattering and groaning. Its detector systems flickered and sparked, not working properly. But it had detected something.

With a pulse of energy, the turret fired its missile into the sky. Smoke streamed from an access hatch on the missile turret as its long-dormant systems began to fail.

Other colonists, rushing out in response to the strange noise, were astonished to see that the military hardware still functioned at all.

"Could've been a misfire," the mayor said. "We should have deactivated that a long time ago."

The projectile shot upward like an exploding javelin, cruising in a smooth, perfect arc until it struck something that looked like a ripple and a halo in the air.

But Octavia stretched her forefinger toward the sky. "No, look! It's hit something."

With a flicker, the observer's cloaking field broke down, and the damaged drone wavered through the sky, its hull split open, one of its three wing covers blown away. Losing altitude, the device spun and sputtered until it crashed like an unwieldy bullet into one of the roughly tilled fields outside of town.

Without even looking to see if the other settlers were following, Octavia ran out to the crash site, where she found a bowl-shaped crater gouged into the dirt. The twisted, blackened wreckage had slammed into the ground. There was very little of the observer left to examine.

Studying what was left of the object while the colonists rushed to join her, Octavia noticed the strange alien markings on the outer covering of the drone, the broken angled panels over the sensor arrays, the large central eye.

"Either the Confederacy has changed its designs an awful lot, or that's nothing a terran ever built," Mayor Nik announced, stating aloud what everyone else had already realized.

Octavia felt a stab of ice inside her. First the storm and earthquake had exposed the huge buried artifact. Now, from out of the sky, an invisible alien device had been shot down—though what its purpose might be she could only guess.

The colonists began to mutter uneasily, looking down at the crashed object. Octavia turned away from the alien wreckage and bit her lower lip, wondering what could possibly be going on here. And what could possibly happen next.

CHAPTER 11

WHEN THE DISTANT ARTIFACT'S INSISTENT SIGNAL reached the zerg swarms on Char, it sent a shockwave like a mental avalanche through the Queen of Blades. As she sat in her growing hive, the pulsing transmission hammered Sarah Kerrigan's temples with an electromagnetic shriek. Somehow this blaring call was attuned to the new resonances in her head, the genetic reception signal that had been incorporated into the zerg from the primal foundation of their DNA.

The thrumming signal caused her hive's organic shell to shimmer, as it too received the long-forgotten awakening call. The exoskeletal material that made up the hive walls began to resonate in response.

Around her, zerg minions reacted with frenzy as the signal triggered some instinctive memory deep inside. The monstrous hydralisks reared up, hissing and slashing with their claws, their pointed spines extruded, ready to fire a rain of deadly darts at any creature they perceived as an enemy.

The doglike zerglings went wild, streaming about and attacking drones and larvae, tearing them to shreds. The alien signal pounded in Kerrigan's head, but she gritted her teeth and imposed order upon her mind. With all of her psi power, she reached out and attempted to control the instincts of her zerglings. She needed to stop them from killing more members of her hive.

In her earlier life, she had been trained in the Confederacy's ghost program. The terrans had given her agonizing neural processing treatments to pacify her latent psi powers. They had surgically implanted a psychic dampener to control her, to make her into a good espionage and intelligence agent. Sarah Kerrigan had been forced to murder countless enemies and learned to treat life itself as a fleeting, disposable commodity.

It had been good training for her. But Kerrigan had been betrayed by the humans she served, who had left her for dead on the zerg-infested battlefield of Tarsonis. The woman who had been Sarah Kerrigan became the Queen of Blades, and she alone held the future of the zerg.

If she could control them.

The signal continued, relentless. From the outer regions of the spreading hive, she could hear the vibrating bellows of an ultralisk as it roared its confusion and fear. She calmed the mammoth-sized monster, then moved on to other minions that were causing too much destruction. With an iron hand, she forced discipline upon her hive again.

Finally the pulsing signal-scream stopped. Blessed, frightening silence fell like an avalanche onto the hive. Kerrigan drew a deep breath, letting her biological systems settle, feeling the hive return to a normal, but still agitated, state. Then she began to think.

The transmitted siren song spoke to some involuntary instinctive memory that the xel'naga had planted inside them. The Queen of Blades knew deep within her own mutated body that the origin of this signal must be incredibly ancient, designed by the same race that had created the protoss and the zerg.

Though she used much of her mind to keep watch on the restless race of the zerg—billions upon billions of creatures—she let part of her thoughts ponder what she had experienced. She knew that the zerg must investigate—must *possess*—whatever had sent this powerful signal.

Finally reaching a decision, Kerrigan summoned all the components of the finest new brood she had assembled after the destruction of the Overmind. She had a mission for Kukulkan Brood, which she had named after the powerful Mayan feathered serpent god from the ancient terran legends. She considered the title to be fearsome and fitting. Kukulkan Brood was one of the most fearsome assault swarms in the scattered zerg race. She could depend on them.

When Kukulkan Brood was assembled, with all its overlords, mutalisks, hydralisks, zerglings, ultralisks, queens, and drones—everything necessary for an impressive assault force—Kerrigan dispatched them from the smoking ruins of Char to fly across space like deadly insects.

Her orders, made perfectly clear even to the murky minds of the various zerg minions, were to find the object that had sent the signal—and take possession of it at all costs.

CHAPTER 12

THE FREE HAVEN MEETING HALL WAS CROWDED once again with confused and disgruntled colonists. This time, though, they needed no one to tell them that things were changing on Bhekar Ro. Things that could affect their lives. Things over which they had no control.

And this time, with the exception of a few children too young to understand what was going on, every colonist was there, even families from outlying farmsteads.

Octavia sat in the front row close to the speaking platform. Many of the younger colonists had chosen to sit near her for support, including Jon, Gregor, Wes, and Kiernan and Kirsten Warner. On Octavia's right sat Cyn McCarthy. The young woman's copper hair hung limply around her somber face as if she had not washed it for several days. And the usual optimism had faded from her dark blue eyes; that scared Octavia the most.

Octavia could sense that the worst of the crisis was yet to come. The Bhekar Ro colonists would need every gram of stubbornness and determination they could muster to get through it. When Mayor Nikolai hopped onto the speaking platform, Octavia was surprised at how quickly the room quieted.

"Now then, we're tough people, and we've been through a lot," he began. "And for a long time we've prided ourselves on being just about unshakable. We deal with weather disasters, tectonic disturbances, plagues, and unexpected deaths, taking it all in stride and moving on. But in the last few days we've seen some things that fall completely outside our understanding. In all our years on Bhekar Ro, we've never had the need to deal with hostile aliens. In other words, we need to prepare for the unexpected."

Rastin the prospector stood up. "Kind of ridiculous to say that, don't you think, Mayor Nik? How can we prepare if we don't know what we're preparing for?"

Shayna Bradshaw spoke next. "If you mean we need to defend ourselves, we don't have any decent weapons. We're colonists—we've got field implements and the occasional projectile gun for shooting game." She gave an emphatic nod of her head. "Not that this planet has any game worth shooting!"

Anger flared in Octavia. "First a huge artifact disintegrates my brother and then sends a beam out into space. Then our missile turret comes to life and shoots an alien object out of the sky. It could be a message, a weapon, or a spy. We need to prepare for an emergency. That weird transmission has attracted some attention, and we don't know what's coming next. So I suggest we start thinking about what we *can* do and stop whining about what we don't know or don't have."

As Octavia subsided onto the bench beside her friends, she was surprised to see Cyn rise to her feet. "What about those terrans you contacted, Nik? Can we expect help from them? Aren't they coming soon?"

A perplexed frown creased Mayor Nikolai's forehead. "The Terran Dominion, ah, yes. Their emperor said he would send someone immediately." He thought for a moment and then flushed. "Of course, that was days ago. And even if they're on their way, we don't know if they'll arrive before the next alien thing shows up in the sky over our heads."

Cyn straightened her shoulders, and Octavia saw a look of fierce determination sparkling in her eyes. "In that case, we'll just have to get ready to fend for ourselves."

Kiernan Warner stood now. "What about the explosives we use for leveling fields and for mining? Couldn't we use those as some sort of weapon?"

A murmur of approval and hope rippled through the room. Wes bounced to his feet. "Hey, and most of us own pulse pistols that we use for hunting lizards."

His cousin Jon stood next. "I'm pretty good with machinery. Maybe between us, Octavia and I can do something about fixing the missile turret in the main square."

Octavia shot him an approving grin. Things were getting better by the moment. "My robo-harvester has a boulder-blaster on it, and a lot of the others have flamethrower attachments. Those could do some pretty significant damage."

Old Rastin interrupted the flow of positive suggestions. "You're all a bunch of lame-brained vespene wasters, if you ask me. Half-buried artifacts, alien ships—are you really convinced we're being invaded? Who do you think these aliens are, anyway? Truth is, we don't know what's going on, and until we do, I'm not gonna sit around here on my butt just yakkin' about it." He pushed past several people toward the exit. "And don't expect me to be givin' all of you free vespene gas just because y'all think the sky is falling." He gave a grunt of disgust, stalked to the exit, and let himself out.

Mayor Nikolai stood for a moment open-mouthed at the old man's audacity before pulling himself together. "Well, of course we shouldn't panic. Mr. Rastin has a point. After all, Emperor Mengsk of the Terran Dominion has been apprised of the situation, and help is probably on its way . . ." His voice trailed off.

Unwilling to see the settlers slip back into complacency, Octavia stepped up onto the platform beside the mayor. "Nik's right. This is not a time to panic. It's time to do something constructive." She smiled as

Cyn and her other friends joined her on the platform to show their support. "We've all heard some things we can do to prepare ourselves for what might be coming."

The crowd rumbled its approval and headed back out toward their homes and farms.

CHAPTER 13

ON THE BRIDGE DECK OF THE *QEL'HA*, EXECUTOR Koronis studied the high-resolution images in fascinated silence. The observer drone transmitted view after view of the magnificent organic structure. The curves and angles gave the uncovered artifact the appearance of a cathedral built by overambitious insects. Swirls and curves, glowing lights, an obviously complex, unfathomable design.

Judicator Amdor stood beside him, radiating excitement and eagerness—a great change from the dour skepticism he had shown for the past several years of their fruitless search.

Koronis was fascinated to see the jagged shards of transparent gleaming rock that protruded from the rubbled terrain all around the exposed object. "Those are Khaydarin crystals," he said, trying to imagine the sheer power that fragments of such size would possess. He recalled the tingle of energy he experienced whenever he touched the tiny shard he kept in his private quarters. Even without the secrets of the strange artifact, massive crystals such as these would be an important weapon and resource for the protoss.

Amdor seemed more intrigued by the strange shapes and runes marked around the outer shell. "Those clues, plus the original encrypted signal, are undeniable proof that this object had its origin with the Wanderers from Afar. We have found a legacy of the Xel'Naga."

The judicator shed his blazing glare upon all the other protoss on the *Qel'Ha*'s bridge. His mental being thrummed with enthusiasm, which affected the other Khalai, inspiring them to greater fervor. "We must retrieve this treasure left by our forefathers, the Xel'Naga." Acting as if he were the commander of the fleet, Amdor gestured forward. "Proceed with all possible haste! We must take possession of this artifact and preserve it for our people."

Executor Koronis stiffened. Amdor had no place in the caste hierarchy to give such an order. So he repeated the order himself, as if the instructions had come from him all along. "We will not be going home immediately. Yes, even though Aiur has suffered in a terrible war, a discovery such as this may help the First Born rise again."

Amdor stared down at the images once more. "The zerg infestation encroaches upon protoss space, and though they share our origin with the Xel'Naga, we First Born can never accept them as brethren. We dare not allow the zerg to capture this artifact or any knowledge it contains. The legacy of the xel'naga must belong to us."

The distant observer continued its survey, sending fresh images of the unremarkable world of Bhekar Ro. Executor Koronis was surprised to see the organized terran colony and the structures erected by the small group of human settlers trying to scrape out an existence there.

However, when the old missile turret activated itself and shot the cloaked drone out of the sky, the executor reared back in his command seat as if the shot had been fired at him personally. The blast incinerated the delicate sensors on the observer's wide arrays, and the reconnaissance drone crashed.

The loss of the observer annoyed Judicator Amdor—not because of any insignificant terran threat, but because he would receive no more images of the xel'naga artifact until their ship arrived at the colony world.

"Once we reach the planet, perhaps we should proceed with caution," Koronis said. "We do not know how much military prowess these terrans have, or what sort of defenses they can mount against us. I suggest we drop our fleet back and enter the system more slowly so that we can reassess the situation."

Now the judicator turned his ire on Koronis. "Unnecessary! You saw the images. It's a fledgling colony, with only a few scraps of technology. Besides, they are human. Terrans are irrelevant."

Koronis conceded the point, and the *Qel'Ha*

launched forward along with the rest of the expeditionary force, streaking through space at the highest speed possible.

The executor reviewed the images the observer had transmitted, staring down at the haunting, fascinating xel'naga structure. After missing the great battle to protect Aiur and failing in their search to find the dark templar, Koronis believed that this artifact could accomplish the third part of their mission. Perhaps this would be a redemption for him.

CHAPTER 14

OVER THE NEXT COUPLE OF DAYS, WHILE THE colonists prepared for another impending emergency, Octavia found herself growing more and more restless. The tension at the back of her mind kept growing. She felt a presence there, as if something alive were trying to communicate with her.

Another premonition? Or just her imagination?

If not for the strange events of the past week, she might have dismissed the uneasy feeling, but she knew it was more than that. She still mourned the loss of her brother Lars, but it was not his ghost or his presence that hovered so insistently at the edge of her awareness.

The tension continued to build like slow psychic pressure until it became unbearable. She worked her fields alone. She had already gathered her small hand weapons and donated what spare food supplies she had to the community kitchen Abdel Bradshaw was organizing.

There had been no sign of reinforcements from the Terran Dominion, and no one in the colony had reported any alien ships or artifacts.

But still, the dread and uneasiness hammered at her mind, making her jump at shadows.

Finally Octavia could take it no more. Hardly knowing what she intended to do, she climbed into the robo-harvester and set off toward the artifact. She needed to see it again, confront it somehow, and find some answers.

All the way there she felt a thread, a growing connection to the thing at a subconscious, almost telepathic level. *Could the artifact itself be alive?*

With each clank of the robo-harvester's heavy treads, she could feel it, hear it. Something sleeping, stirring. Something enormous and alien.

It had seemed to devour Lars—absorb him, perhaps—and then it had seemed to find him wanting. *Yes,* the presence in her mind seemed to say. It hungered. It needed to feed on life.

But not terran life. Something . . . different.

As the robo-harvester descended into the second valley and rolled across the basin toward the slope where the artifact lay half unburied, the feeling of hunger grew stronger, more insistent. Hunger for life.

Angrily, Octavia tried to push the presence out of her head. If it didn't want terran life, why had it killed her brother? The thing had casually murdered him and then—what? Discarded his essence? She didn't know, and it no longer mattered to her. All that mattered was that Lars was dead because of this thing.

She brought the robo-harvester to a halt at the base of the slope and stared at the enormous, eerie artifact with a hard, calculating gaze. Hungry, was it? Well, she had a hunger too—for vengeance. And she needed to do something practical for a change.

From the cockpit of the robo-harvester she powered up the boulder-blaster. She herself had suggested at the town meeting that it could be used as a weapon. Well, now she was going to find out.

Octavia took careful aim and triggered the small explosive launcher that was normally reserved for clearing boulders from fields. She held on and watched, already feeling satisfied.

The blast struck its target dead on. The familiar explosion was loud and powerful, smashing many of the tall crystals that grew like weeds in the rubble. A rain of pebbles and dirt pattered around the robo-harvester for nearly a full minute.

When Octavia was sure the shower of dirt was over, she cleared the robo-harvester's windshield and peered out to survey the damage she had done.

There was none. Not a scratch.

If anything, the artifact appeared glossier . . . *healthier* than before. Octavia had only succeeded in clearing more caked soil from its exterior. As she stared in frustrated fascination, the artifact began to pulse. The forest of surrounding crystals lit with an inner fire. Crackling energy skittered across the smooth, sinuous surface of the thing, flashing and growing in intensity until threads of lightning wove themselves together into a solid beam that speared out at the robo-harvester.

She yelled and ducked, covering her eyes.

The retaliatory bolt hit the heavy vehicle like a meteor. Octavia grabbed the seat inside the cab and held on as the robo-harvester rocked on its treads. She wanted to dive outside for cover, but decided that might be even more dangerous.

The vehicle's control panels sparked and sizzled. The alien artifact continued its pummeling lightning blast, as if to make certain its message was received. Octavia's hair lifted away from her head, alive with static electricity. She let out another loud yell, halfway between a panicked scream and a curse, at the towering object in the cliffside.

Finally the blast ended, leaving her half deafened and the big machine completely dead. Her eyes swam with brilliant smears of color from the dazzling lights. Ozone and smoke filled the cabin, and crackling steam drifted up from the harvester's engine compartment.

Octavia scrambled out of the cab, burning her hands and the side of one leg on the hot metal. In awe, she backed away from the damaged vehicle. She could tell by looking at it that there would be no way to repair the behemoth. The electrical systems were completely gone, and many of the moving parts had fused. The vehicle would never start.

But at least she was alive.

The artifact had destroyed the robo-harvester, though it had not harmed her, even after she had knowingly attacked it. What did it mean? Octavia shook her head and chided herself for having tried something so foolish.

Running a hand through her brown curls, she looked behind her at the sun lowering toward the horizon. It would be a long, long walk home.

CHAPTER 15

AS HER SHIP MOVED THROUGH THE VOID OF space, the dark templar Xerana sat surrounded by her intellectual resources, the library and museum she had compiled. Her treasures.

She had no need for sleep now that she had a mystery in her grasp.

Xerana had received and recorded the loud signal from the distant and unremarkable world. She had studied the transmission, searching for nuances, trying to decode it. She took the ancient, incomprehensible electromagnetic patterns and organized them into layers of subtle meaning. She doubted many others alive in the entire galaxy would be able to fathom such things.

But the dark templar scholars had access to resources and arcane xel'naga texts. She knew scraps of history that the rest of the protoss had forgotten long ago. Xerana alone, among all her race, had the best chance of deciphering the true meaning and origin of this alien transmission.

She let her ship drift, allowing the currents of the Void to carry it wherever the vagaries of gravity and solar wind and space might direct it. She played the signal over and over until every cell of her body was awash with the pulsing rhythms, until her mind was filled with the hypnotic tone—and finally, using every shred of knowledge she had in her archives, Xerana was able to comprehend the deep secret of the strange awakening object.

Roused at last from her obsessive concentration, the dark templar scholar felt the thrill of understanding surge through her body. But as she made her way toward the bridge of her wandering vessel, she felt weak and shaky. Xerana paused a moment to marshal her energies. She had so much to do, a mission to accomplish. Then she hurried to her controls and sank into the guidance chair, feeling as if she had become one with her craft.

Though she had translated the mysterious signal, Xerana also knew that other protoss—and perhaps even zerg—would have heard the beacon, too. But none of them would understand what the artifact *was*.

She had no choice but to do her duty.

Long ago, the Judicator Conclave had ostracized the dark templar. Although her people had been exiled from Aiur, driven away from the rest of their race and persecuted, Xerana and her comrades maintained their loyalty. Even now, honor required her to bear a warning, no matter the cost to herself.

Xerana powered up the engines of her scout vessel

and set off at reckless speed into the emptiness, navigating toward the coordinates she had traced as the origin of the signal. Aside from her knowledge and her confidence, she had few weapons.

She traveled alone, fully aware that other protoss might even now be converging on the site. Any judicator would be eager to capture a dark templar like herself. This journey would be very dangerous for her, but Xerana had no time for fear. She had no choice but to take the risk.

Her vessel rapidly closed the distance to Bhekar Ro.

CHAPTER 16

DISPATCHED FROM CHAR, KUKULKAN BROOD traveled across the empty vacuum between the stars. Even out in the cold darkness, their armored bodies turned the zerg into a fleet of monstrous living spaceships. Groups of different creatures controlled by numerous overlords, the Brood followed the directives of the Queen of Blades, who had envisioned this scheme to investigate, capture, and exploit the xel'naga artifact.

It would belong to the zerg by right of conquest.

Massive behemoths flew under their own energy, like star-spanning manta rays, the largest creatures ever known in the charted galaxy. With superdense hides, the behemoths could contain many other zerg minions within the folds and pockets of their sprawling bodies. These creatures had no weapons, not even any defenses, but they carried the full strength and horror of all the zerg subspecies.

Ages ago, when the ancient xel'naga tinkerers had

experimented with creating the zerg, they had adapted the ferocious and highly competitive indigenous life-forms on the planet Zerus. These prototype zerg had rapidly adapted and assimilated all of the native species there, and as their race grew more powerful and more intelligent, the fledgling zerg Overmind had reached a critical point, a roadblock that prevented it from expanding further. The zerg were planet-bound—until the star-sailing behemoths had wandered into the system.

Immense and docile creatures of the airless void, the behemoths drifted close enough that the Overmind had called out to them with its great telepathic powers. After it had lured the unsuspecting life-forms within reach, the zerg minions had attacked and infested them. Before long, the genetic plan of the starfaring behemoths had been incorporated into the zerg DNA.

Thus, the fearsome zerg developed the ability to travel from star system to star system. They became unstoppable.

Now, after being dispatched by the Queen of Blades, the behemoths of Kukulkan Brood carried Sarah Kerrigan's strike force to Bhekar Ro. The huge creatures converged in orbit, an organic cloud that blotted out the light from distant suns. They descended lower to the veiled fringes of the atmosphere, scraping tendrils of air as their skins opened up to disgorge the overlords, the main carriers of the zerg forces.

The overlords were immense creatures, exoskeleton-armored carriers shaped like ridged crustaceans with enormous mandibles and dangling claws. But even so they were dwarfed by the sprawling flesh of the leviathans in the sky overhead. The overlords emerged from carrying pouches and dropped in freefall through the thickening atmosphere and buffeting winds.

Since the xel'naga artifact had only briefly broadcast its compelling beacon, the zerg did not know the precise location, only a general area. But the overlords of Kukulkan Brood were patient and very thorough. Under their own power, they cruised through greasy clouds and patches of thunderstorms, scratched by lightning but unharmed.

Finally the spreading swarm arrived in the vicinity of the large artifact. Only a small portion of the Brood remained in orbit with the leviathans, a second wave prepared to descend once the first monstrous troops had accomplished their objective.

The overlords spread out, seeking to release groups of drones that would establish numerous hatcheries and then several creep colonies. The heart of the new zerg colony, the hatchery would generate enough larvae to spawn all the minions Kukulkan Brood would need to take over this planet.

The overlords would overwhelm the mysterious artifact itself and seize what could be taken. But first, in preparation, they intended to find local victims, organisms that the zerg could infest, and thereby increase their numbers . . .

*   *   *

Though he had set up his dwelling and his gas refineries over the vespene geysers, far from the town, the old prospector Rastin had been seeing too much of people for the past week. First Lars and Octavia Bren had come by to get more fuel, then he'd been called into Free Haven for not one but two all-colony meetings.

He had grudgingly driven his only vehicle—a clunky old field crawler—into town. That was more socialization than he liked to do in a year. On both occasions he'd stayed for only a few hours before driving back to his refineries and his dog, Old Blue.

But after the last storm and earthquake, one of his three remaining geysers had given out, and no matter how much he poked and probed and kicked at his machinery, he could not get the thing functioning again. He had heard that there were several new geysers over the ridge and into the next valley, but Rastin had lived in the same place for almost forty years and just didn't have the gumption to pack up his belongings and move out there.

Although the idea of being even farther away from Free Haven had its appeal . . .

Old Blue came out from his cool resting spot under the corrugated porch and sniffed around. The big mutated mastiff stood almost as tall as his master's chest. Rastin had originally hoped to turn the horse-like canine, with its bristly blue fur and an appetite like an elephant, into a beast of burden. Man's best friend combined with a draft animal to haul mineral samples and supplies. Instead, the dog was just a companion, a big, lovable creature that drooled a lot and growled occasionally, but never meant it.

Rastin distractedly patted the dog, who galloped around looking for urchin lizards or crab beetles to chase. Once he'd gotten a muzzleful of needles from an urchin lizard, and the dog knew better than to bite when he played.

Rastin banged at the refinery equipment with his worn old tools, grumbling and cursing the engines. But the machinery was not impressed, even with his harshest language. He stood in disgust, hurled his spanner wrench off into the rocks as far as it would go, then berated himself for doing such a stupid thing, because now he'd have to go fetch it.

Beside him, he was surprised when Old Blue sat on his haunches and howled up at the sky. The big blue dog's lips curled back, exposing his teeth as he growled and then whined.

"Now what?" Rastin said. "You afraid of a little mound-hopper again, you big sissy?"

But Old Blue did not calm down. He continued to growl, then lowered himself on all fours and began to wriggle backward, as if to slink away. Rastin looked up and saw a swarm of shapes in the sky, a flock of creatures—unbelievably large creatures—descending through the clouds and moving like an armada of organic battleships. "What the—?"

With an ominous buzzing sound like a hive of infuriated wasps, the swarm of invaders came down, dozens of armored and multilegged creatures that split apart, some of them descending toward the foothills where Rastin made his home.

The vespene geysers continued to boil and steam into the air, advertising their resources. They seemed to attract the strange alien invaders. Old Blue yelped and finally ran out of canine courage. He bolted back under the corrugated porch to hide in the shadows.

Summoning his surly anger to combat a paralyzing blast of fear, Rastin lunged into his shack and grabbed an old blunderbuss projectile launcher, a pellet weapon that he used for picking off rodents that ate too many of his stores. He came out and held up the weapon, gritting his teeth in defiance.

The zerg overlords dropped low over the foothills, approaching the vital vespene geysers. Their carapaces cracked open and released a rain of hideous monsters that seemed to be all spines and armored exoskeletons and clacking jaws. As the zerglings poured out in a stampede of vicious claws and fangs, Rastin stood his ground for a moment, then backed toward his shack.

Behind the overlords, a new type of creature descended—a mass of thrashing armored tentacles, a sinuous head, and a stretched skin membrane that extended like bat wings to connect some of the tentacles.

A queen. And it seemed intent on coming directly toward him.

Rastin discharged his first round of hot metal pellets

into the oncoming swarm, reloaded, and fired again. He knew his weapon was too weak, knew that in a thousand years he could never find enough ammunition to fight off this threat, but he swore and fired again. And again. When he had no pellets left, he hurled curses as the ravenous zerglings swept toward him like a tidal wave of death.

And then they were upon him.

CHAPTER 17

OCTAVIA DID NOT LIKE TO BE OUT ON FOOT AT night, but with the robo-harvester unable to function, she had no choice but to walk. She traversed the many kilometers across the valley, climbed up over the ridge panting and sweating, skipped through the scree, and stumbled her way back down toward the colony town.

She hated every second of it.

The ground was uncertain, full of shadows and hidden potholes, crevices between rocks that seemed to reach out and grab her feet. If she twisted an ankle, she would have to limp all the way back to Free Haven.

The night was dark, the skies murky and overcast. Clouds smothered the stars, but at least they held no storms. Strange flashes of light rippled across the sky like auroras or distant lightning, but the colors and energy patterns were different from the exotic weather fronts she normally witnessed on Bhekar Ro.

Too many strange things were happening lately.

She increased her pace down through the foothills, glad to see the dim lights of old Rastin's vespene refinery. The reclusive prospector probably wouldn't welcome company, especially this late at night, but Octavia had no choice. He had a vehicle, a Vespene-powered field crawler that had endured for decades. Maybe he could give her a ride into town.

If nothing else, Old Blue would be happy to see her, and after the miserable times she had just endured, it would be a relief just to pat his bristly fur and see his thick tail wag with delight.

She stumbled onto a path the hermit must have used. With relief she worked her way down toward the homestead, feeling a spring in her step from the hope that her ordeal might be over soon.

As she approached, Octavia saw only a few automatic lights burning around the refinery superstructures, lending a strange silvery glow to the vespene geysers that curled into the air. The place seemed abandoned, haunted . . . Perhaps old Rastin had already gone to bed. She had no idea what time it was.

"Hello, Rastin?" she called. "It's Octavia Bren." She paused, but only silence answered her. Even the fiddler beetles and the throaty humming lizards were silent in the night—which was very strange. It made the darkness seem more oppressive.

"Hello, Rastin? I need your help."

Although she normally would have walked up to

his door and pounded, this uncharacteristic silence made her uneasy. Reclusive Rastin was unpredictable at times, and it wasn't hard to imagine that he might come out with his weapon to "defend" his home against late-night intruders. She didn't want to get a backside full of rodent shot.

She drew closer, her eagerness dwindling. "Hello? Is anybody home?" At least she expected Old Blue to start barking at her. If anything, the silence grew heavier.

She wondered if perhaps Mayor Nik had called another colony meeting. In that case, Rastin might have gone to the village, taking Old Blue with him. Yes, that was probably the answer.

When she saw his vehicle sitting by itself in a clearing not far from his shack, she knew her explanation was wrong. The old man never went anywhere without his vehicle, so he must be home. This didn't make any sense at all. Her stomach filled with the ice of growing dread.

Inside her head, she felt a rising static, an echoing clamor of countless alien voices, discrete entities but somehow all the same. Her skin crawled. What did it mean? She had felt something similar—the strange background hubbub of an alien presence—back at the buried artifact that had disintegrated Lars and wrecked her robo-harvester.

But this was . . . different somehow. More evil. Menacing. Hungry.

Approaching the prospector's dwelling, she saw

that the broken rocky ground was now covered with a creeping film, thick and slimy like a carpet of biomass. The substance was an organic growing mat that spread out from the vespene geysers, the refinery, and the shack itself.

She bent down to touch it and was immediately sorry. Her fingers felt soiled, as if she'd never be able to wipe the feeling off. The creeping mat smelled of rot and decay, unlike any vegetation that had ever grown here on Bhekar Ro. The carpet of biomass flexed and grew and expanded even as she watched.

On bare patches of dirt where the growing mat had not yet spread, she saw scratches—sharp, clawed footprints of several varieties, as if a mob of insectlike monsters had swarmed over the site.

Concern for Rastin overcame her fear, and she tiptoed closer to the prospector's house. Silence still reigned. She called out one more time, ready to run as her deep-seated uneasiness swelled to a terror pitch.

"Rastin? Please answer me."

As she stepped on the creaking sheet of corrugated metal that formed the porch, she heard something stir beneath it and saw a large creature moving in the shadows. "Old Blue!" she called, mentally telling herself to be relieved, though she felt no decrease in tension.

She backed away when she saw a flash of matted sky-blue fur and rippling muscles as the beast hauled itself out from the shadows where it lurked. And though it had once been Old Blue, the giant mutated dog was now something else entirely.

It was *infested.*

Spines thrust from its back. Above each leg, jointed, armored limbs sprouted from its shoulders, ending in clacking claws. Old Blue's original eyes had sunken in, and a new set—four of them—protruded on waving stalks, sweeping around to focus on Octavia. It curled its lips back, showing fangs that had grown into tusks. The drool that boiled out of its rabid mouth was thick and gelatinous, like a green acidic slime.

Now Octavia heard more things stirring around the homestead, bodies moving about. The dog-thing made a deep liquid roar in its throat, and Octavia stumbled away. Old Blue's paws split open to reveal a new set of claws as large as scimitars, and its muscles coiled like well-oiled pulleys and cables.

Octavia turned to run into the darkness. Old Blue lunged after her.

CHAPTER 18

THE PLANET DID NOT LOOK LIKE MUCH AS THE *Qel'Ha* approached, flanked by the protoss expeditionary fleet. But appearances hardly mattered. Right now Executor Koronis was interested only in the origin of the signal that had summoned the protoss here. The xel'naga message.

Judicator Amdor stood beside him, glaring out the viewports with his orange-yellow eyes. He seemed to believe he could conquer the blistered brown-and-green world below through sheer force of will alone.

"I want no failures, Executor. Not this time," Amdor said sternly, his telepathic message sloppy enough that others on the flagship's bridge could hear the undertone of threat. This annoyed Koronis. Bad for morale.

Smug in their position of political and religious power, judicators often did not understand how the rest of the Khalai responded to undercurrents and subtleties. But Koronis would not provoke a confrontation now. Such matters were better dealt with behind telepathic shielded walls, so that even the loudest arguments and mental shouts could not be picked up by others aboard the ship.

That conflict could wait until later. He had a more important mission now.

"We will maintain a defensive fleet in orbit," he said. "Three carriers will track our position from the high ground while the rest will descend to claim the xel'naga object. We do not know if we will encounter any resistance." He looked around the bridge, felt the excitement and loyalty thrumming through his crew.

"I will send scouts first to clear out any resistance, while shuttles will follow immediately behind to carry our zealots, dragoons, and enough reavers to maintain supremacy on the ground. Judicator Amdor and I will ride down in the lead arbiter, while other judicators will take twenty more arbiters and provide shields and cloaking cover for our forces."

Amdor looked annoyed that the executor had not consulted him first, but nodded his smooth, grayish head, agreeing with his own role in the important operation.

Like falcons, the scouts separated from the remainder of the fleet in space and streaked down through the atmosphere of Bhekar Ro. Aboard the high-speed fighters, dual photon blasters and batteries of antimatter missiles were armed and ready for resistance.

Executor Koronis hoped such an aggressive posture would prove to be an unnecessary precaution, since he was sure his fleet had arrived here first, before any enemies could have responded to the artifact's beacon. He moved from his command bridge, followed briskly by the tall and imposing form of Judicator Amdor. They marched down the flagship corridors to the launching bays. Koronis climbed aboard the lead arbiter.

When the ships were launched, flying in the wakes of the fast scouts, Koronis's arbiter ship dropped away from his fleet, the executor feeling uneasy at parting with the magnificent carrier *Qel'Ha*. It looked like a long, smooth pod in space, an ellipsoid split into half-closed petals. The executor had been aboard the giant flagship for decades in his fruitless search, and now his impending triumph, the end of their hunt for knowledge, was tempered by a dim sense of foreboding. Somehow he didn't believe this mission would be as simple as the judicator claimed it would be.

He transmitted instructions that the descending fleet was to avoid contact with the not-too-distant terran colony. He had no fear of any weapons or defenses the settlers might bring to bear, but he had learned not to ask for trouble. Koronis avoided distractions and conflicts, concentrating on what was necessary to accomplish his objective.

Surrounded by their blanket of invisibility, the arbiters, dropships, carriers, and scouts swooped down into the stark valley at the foot of the exposed artifact. Mineral outcroppings and a fresh field of sputtering vespene geysers showed Koronis that he'd have the resources necessary to build all the reavers, photon cannons, and local defenses he would need.

After the arbiters had landed, looking like beetles with broad carapaces, most of the protoss remained aboard, giving Executor Koronis the honor of being the first to set foot on the soon-to-be-conquered world.

To Koronis the air smelled dry and gritty, as if too much rock dust hung in the air. He paused, just *feeling* the place. Judicator Amdor strode up beside him so that the two of them stood together at the base of the slope where the massive exposed face of the mysterious xel'naga artifact filled the mountainside.

"Magnificent!" Amdor said, his knobby headgear gleaming in the diluted light. "Can you feel the power? Can you sense how great our victory will be when we return to Aiur?" His hands clenched into fists.

The judicator stepped forward and raised his long arms, extending his hands in an all-encompassing gesture. His dark robes curled around his body like a living thing. "I claim this worthy object for the First Born. It is a triumph for the protoss. Let no one doubt our sole possession. *En taro Adun!*"

Executor Koronis knitted his craggy brows, thinking that Amdor was premature in his celebration. *"En taro Adun,"* he responded. He ran his fingers down his long sash of office. Yes, acquiring this amazing artifact was a glorious accomplishment, but he wondered what the strict judicator bureaucracy would do with it. And how would they excavate something so huge and bring it back to war-ravaged Aiur?

Then, from the arbiter he had commanded, Koronis heard a desperate signal transmitted on a tight telepathic band. It was templar Mess'Ta aboard the *Qel'Ha*. "Executor Koronis! We have detected a large fleet of zerg behemoths in orbit, coming around the rim of the planet. They were hiding on the night side! The zerg have arrived here first."

Koronis immediately assessed the threat even as Judicator Amdor reeled with anger at the affront of the enemy invaders.

"What is the strength of the zerg fleet?" he asked.

"A complete Brood, Executor—as many minions as we have ever seen. This is no simple scout force, but a full-scale invasion."

Koronis remained grim, and Judicator Amdor turned to him, eyes blazing. "They must have responded to the signal as well! Executor, we must not lose possession of this xel'naga artifact. The protoss will defend this."

Koronis transmitted back to Mess'Ta, "You know what to do, templar."

"Yes, Executor. Defenses mounted. Flights of interceptors prepared and targeted. I have given orders to engage the enemy."

CHAPTER 19

AS SHE STOOD FACING THE INFESTED MONSTER, Octavia hoped that some primitive part of Old Blue's brain would recognize her and hesitate. But that hope was dashed in an instant as the huge dog-thing lunged.

She ducked and rolled off the corrugated porch so that the giant slavering monstrosity leaped over her. Its additional angular limbs thrashed and flailed to grab her. The razor-sharp claws along its back clacked, slicing the air. The eye stalks protruding from its head swiveled to watch her so the blue-furred dog could see where to strike next.

Her exhaustion and despair forgotten, Octavia scrambled from the porch, tearing open her hands on the rusty corrugated metal. The dog-thing spun about on the broken rocks around Rastin's shack, long claws spraying pebbles.

She ran in the other direction, flying across the stones. "Rastin!" she shouted, but in her heart she already knew that no help would come from the old prospector.

Octavia raced for the meager shelter of the low refinery towers that covered the vespene geysers. The hideous mutation that had once been Old Blue bounded after her, and she put on more speed than she thought she possessed. Her muscles felt tense enough to snap, but somehow adrenaline held her together.

She reached the small refinery structure and ducked between the laced metal bars of the scaffolding just as the canine horror struck the superstructure. He was too large to fit through, and she felt safe for a moment.

Old Blue crashed again against the metal framework, bending the heavy paristeel. Two of his long, spindly arms lashed forward like striking snakes, trying to reach her. Hot spittle and slime splattered against the framework, where it began to sizzle, releasing corrosive foam.

Wasting no energy on a scream, Octavia backed into the refinery piping and controls. As Old Blue tore two girders apart, she found a release nozzle and wrenched it open, blasting the monstrous dog with a mouthful of concentrated, superheated vespene gas.

Howling and roaring, the creature thrashed backward, ripping open its hide on a sharp metal edge.

Seeing her chance, Octavia ran again, this time toward old Rastin's beaten-up vehicle. If only she could get inside and start it . . .

When she was halfway across the gap, sprinting headlong with her eyes fastened on the door latch of the field crawler, she realized that the surly old codger might keep his vehicle locked so that no one else could start it. It seemed impossible and foolish on a small colony such as Free Haven, but Rastin was unpredictable.

Her hand slammed against the door handle—it was unlocked! She wrenched the vehicle open and nearly collapsed with relief. Octavia lurched headfirst into the driver's seat and slammed the door after her.

Old Blue was limping now, either injured or exhausted—or possibly dying from the horrific infestation that crawled through his muscular furred body. The dog-thing came toward her with faltering steps. Powerful jaws snapped and slashed at the air, as if chomping on an unseen enemy. Its spiny outgrowths flailed, as if grasping for something, hungry, wanting to tear apart any object within reach.

Octavia fumbled under the field crawler's steering column and found a starter button. She pressed hard with her thumb.

The engine coughed but did not catch. The vehicle seemed to sigh, as if it had already given up. She punched the starter button again. "Come on!"

Old Blue came closer, weaving, snarling.

Just then, the door of Rastin's shack was torn open from inside, literally ripped from its hinges and thrown to the ground ten feet away. A lumbering hulk strode into the faint light that seeped through the murky darkness. But this one was a humanoid form—or at least it *had* been. The figure looked as if it had been redesigned by a madman who had too many spare parts left over from a variety of species.

Rastin!

Growths and snapping tentacles protruded from the man's ruptured, festering skin. What had been Rastin's face now hung low, sunken into his chest, and the only recognizable features were two wild eyes—agonized, even frightened. But other alien eyes, black and covered with scaly carapaces, peered out from his shoulders and from the top of his skull.

On heavy feet, Rastin plodded forward, his human arms extended, though the muscular bestial limbs thrashed, claws clacking.

Old Blue staggered to a halt near the thin-hulled field crawler. From the way the monster had torn apart the scaffolding around the vespene refinery, Octavia knew that this monster could easily peel away the scant protection. Old Blue could rip her out of the vehicle like the soft meat of a thin-skinned berrynut.

She locked the door anyway.

But the dog-thing collapsed in front of her, seeming to choose its position carefully. Beneath the dog's blue-furred hide, sores began to boil. His hulk expanded, puffing and throbbing. Old Blue raised his distorted head and let out a long, thin whine.

Octavia punched the starter button again. The field crawler's engine ground and ground, picking up speed, humming, almost catching . . .

Rastin careened off the porch of his shack and slogged toward her, arms extended. Old Blue shuddered and let out a last animal howl of pain.

The vehicle's engine finally roared, and Octavia did not wait around. She shifted the field crawler into gear and tore off, spraying stones and gravel, racing away from the trap.

Behind her, Old Blue's infested carcass erupted in an explosion of high-powered gases, flying chunks of meat, and splattering slime. The shock wave from the explosion and the rolling fist of poisonous fumes swept outward and smashed into her vehicle, rocking it sideways and rattling the windows. Luckily, the driver's cabin remained sealed, although gouts of ichor spattered the windows and doors.

Under the onslaught, the capricious engine coughed and almost died, but she coaxed it to life again and roared ahead, escaping Rastin's homestead.

Behind her, the infested prospector stood as if in despair, his unnatural limbs thrashing, his human face wailing with grief for his dead dog.

Octavia pulled away, barely allowing herself to feel safe—and then the ground in front of her swirled and split and boiled, as if giving birth to creatures from the depths of her nightmares.

Two gigantic reptilian monsters surged up from the dry, cracked ground in front of her. They resembled enormous cobras with skeletal heads, fangs like daggers, and blazing eyes that held too much intelligence. The creatures reared back, their rounded carapaces gleaming in the starlight, and moved to flank her. They hissed and rattled as they prepared to strike, reaching out with heavily armored limbs.

Octavia swerved the field crawler from one side to another, amazed at how responsive the innocuous-looking old vehicle was. She sped past the two creatures even as the ground broke and surged behind her. More attackers rose from underground.

With a sound like a thousand air bullets, the creatures bent over and unleashed a volley of long, spear-like spines that slammed into the back of the field crawler. Some of them protruded through the metal body.

Octavia did not dare slow down to check for damage. As she raced off into the night, another volley of the deadly spines peppered the vehicle, making it a pincushion.

With every second, her distance from the vespene refinery increased. She drove blindly into the night, out of the foothills and toward the distant town, eyes wide, throat dry, heart pounding.

It did not yet occur to her that she had survived. She only knew she had to get to Free Haven to warn the rest of the colony. If there was anything left of it.

CHAPTER 20

CHEWING ON IMAGINARY STEEL NAILS—THOUGH
he probably wouldn't have noticed if he'd had actual
hardware between his molars—General Edmund
Duke sat upright in the uncomfortable command
chair of the battlecruiser *Norad III*. He was ready for
action, and so were his men. He had ordered them so.

They had an alien artifact to investigate and helpless colonists to rescue. If they were lucky, the mission
might turn out to be even more than that.

He knew better than to rally his marines by making gruff and patriotic speeches in a misguided
attempt to fire them up enough to put their lives on
the line for Arcturus Mengsk. The general himself
wasn't entirely comfortable with the politics of the
situation, but he tried not to dwell on it too much.
He knew the appropriate carrot to dangle when
he wanted to inspire his troops to give him their
personal best.

"Colony world Bhekar Ro on screen, General,"

said Lieutenant Scott from the tactical station. "Approaching orbital insertion."

General Duke nodded.

"I'm extending our sensor net, General," said Lieutenant Scott. "Scanning ahead for defensive positions."

Duke gave the handsome young officer a smug look, raising both eyebrows. "I figure our fifteen battlecruisers can pretty much take care of any little farming trouble, Lieutenant."

"Sir! Enemy vessels!" the Lieutenant shouted, double-checking his tactical readouts as the battlecruiser fleet homed in on Bhekar Ro.

On the screen he displayed a full analysis of what lurked high above the colony world. The soldiers on board the *Norad III* saw the display and muttered in surprise.

Duke clenched his jaw and leaned forward. "I thought those little slimeballs might be laying an ambush for us." He recognized the smooth-shelled, split-ellipsoidal protoss carriers. The general had never been able to determine whether the ships' mottled discoloration was intentional or just ion stains from generations of service in the rigors of space.

"Power up the fleet's Yamato guns," he said. "We'll go in and ring their bells before anybody even knows we're here."

General Duke smiled and knotted his hands together as if a scrawny enemy throat were clenched between them. "All right, men," he broadcast through the long corridors of the battlecruiser. "Let's go kick some alien butt!"

The men cheered so loudly that the metal hulls rang with their enthusiasm. Alpha Squadron had been born to fight, and Emperor Mengsk had wasted their potential on pointless busywork for far too long. The marines were as bored as the general was.

"Sir, it's unlikely that the protoss fleet was just lying in wait for Alpha Squadron," Lieutenant Scott pointed out. "They have already engaged another opponent."

As they observed, the protoss carriers launched waves of robotic interceptors toward a hideous swarm of insectoid aliens, monstrous creatures that survived in the vacuum of space.

General Duke had seen those awful things before. "The zerg *and* the protoss! By damn, they've made an alliance!"

Then the protoss interceptors smashed into the zerg minions. In seconds, the alien battlefield turned into a chaos of weaponry discharges and exploded hulls.

"I don't think that's much of an alliance, sir," Lieutenant Scott said.

"Fine with me if they tear each other apart," the general growled. "I hate 'em both."

The protoss carriers launched more waves of interceptors that sought out and attacked all of the zerg creatures within reach. At first the robotic interceptors were like a swarm of stinging insects, concentrating on the massive zerg overlords.

Nearby, they made quick work of the crablike guardians, whose ability to hurl corrosive acid would have been devastating against ground targets but who were almost defenseless in space. The interceptors moved fast, striking, destroying, then searching for new targets.

Seeing the carnage, the loss of numerous overlords and guardians, a group of flying zerg creatures known as scourges broke through and attacked the carrier itself. Reckless but determined, the group of scourges careened into the protoss ship and exploded on impact, sacrificing themselves to take out an opposing alien vessel.

Cheering silently at seeing the loss of each protoss craft, General Duke said, "I've had a grudge against those alien bastards ever since Chau Sara." In their first contact ever with the human race, the protoss had come in giant ships and without warning had killed every living thing on the terran colony planet, exterminating millions. General Duke himself had barely escaped from its infested sister planet of Mar Sara, the first place he had ever laid eyes on the hideous zerg. "Serves them all right."

Duke had no love for the zerg either. In fact, he hated all aliens on general principle. And now the zerg and protoss were tearing each other apart in space. He couldn't imagine a more entertaining sight.

As the alien firefight continued in orbit, General Duke narrowed his eyes. He waited a moment, watching the destruction, then a smile crept over his face. "Attention, Alpha Squadron!" His booming voice broadcast through all fifteen battlecruisers. "Battle stations! We're gonna come in with all guns blazing and let them alien bastards have it."

Lieutenant Scott watched the frenzy on his tactical screen. "Sir, shouldn't we wait, send in some reconnaissance to gather tactical data before we make our move?"

The general gestured toward the screen. "You can see with your own eyes, Lieutenant—and I've never been one to sit around on my hindquarters gathering background information when it's time for *action*."

He rose from his hard command chair, knowing that standing would give him a more powerful leadership presence. "Emperor Arcturus Mengsk has declared Bhekar Ro to be of vital terran interest." He worked to keep a straight face, knowing that none of the marines had ever heard of the place before now.

"Therefore, it is our duty to protect the colony and all of its resources from any enemy power. The presence of these alien scumbags can only be interpreted as a threat to the Terran Dominion, and we're not gonna let them endanger a single speck of dust on this colony!"

General Duke ordered all of his ships forward. With the *Norad III* in the vanguard, Alpha Squadron plunged into the fray.

CHAPTER 21

TERRIFIED, BRUISED, AND EXHAUSTED, OCTAVIA had no time to rest or to hesitate. Free Haven was in danger, and adrenaline burned like laser-lightning through her veins.

It was after midnight when Octavia careened past the low barricade fence and down the street into the village. Sounding the alarm, she drove poor Rastin's field crawler directly to Mayor Nikolai's house at the center of town and roused him out of a sound sleep. Despite his bleary eyes and the rumpled state of his spiky blond hair, he came instantly awake as Octavia related what had become of Old Blue and Rastin.

"I don't know what those creatures are, Nik, but they're alien—and they were following me."

He groaned. "Octavia, I've never known you to have an overactive imagination. But how many times have you come running into town now, raising the alarm about aliens?"

She dragged him over to Rastin's field crawler,

where he saw the dozens of poisonous spines pro-truding like a pincushion from the back wall. The last set of monsters had shot them at her. The man could not deny the evidence of his own eyes.

Leaving Octavia to notify the people in the village proper, Mayor Nikolai excused himself and spent the next two hours at the communications station inside his home office, trying to contact families at outlying farms via the short-range comm system.

Octavia rousted Cyn McCarthy as well as Kiernan, Kirsten, Wes, Jon, and Gregor from their beds. She sent the young men out as runners from house to house in Free Haven to let the other colonists know of the approaching danger. Then she ran to the storm siren and turned it on to alert the surrounding farms as quickly as possible, even though they wouldn't know yet what kind of danger they were in until the runners got to them.

By the time the first hundred or so colonists had gathered on the street outside the meeting hall, Octavia was pleased to find that Abdel Bradshaw was already inside. His wife, Shayna, instead of arguing or criticizing, had taken it upon herself to begin setting up cots and laying out medical supplies.

"In case we have wounded," she explained.

Octavia nodded. "Let me know if you need any help."

While Cyn and Kirsten stayed to help the Bradshaws, Octavia went out to the street to speak to the sleepy-eyed colonists. A crowd had gathered around the damaged field crawler, muttering in fear and amazement. A boy of about twelve reached forward to one of the protruding spines, but Octavia snapped at him to stop. "Those could be poisonous!" she said. The others stayed away.

Next, she organized the waiting villagers into task groups, each with a different assignment. She sent a dozen of the younger teens into the meeting hall to take care of the colony's youngest children so that their parents could go about their duties without worrying.

For what felt like hours, Octavia issued orders, answered questions, took suggestions, made snap decisions, and directed traffic as villagers brought supplies and weapons to the central gathering area. She sent Cyn with a work crew to fortify the fences on the perimeter of the village. After a couple of hours, Mayor Nikolai came out of his house, looking very disturbed.

"Did you reach everyone?" Octavia asked.

He frowned. "Most of them, except for thirteen families. Those, I couldn't contact at all."

Octavia's stomach clenched. She had seen what had happened to Rastin and his dog, somehow infested with the alien menace. Had other colonists met the same fate already?

"Maybe a few of them heard the storm siren," she suggested, knowing it was a long shot.

Mayor Nikolai glanced around at the bustling colonists. Although dawn was over an hour away, the village was wide awake and embroiled in frantic activity. "I certainly don't see any of them."

"You've got to keep trying," Octavia said.

Just then, her runners returned from their errands and raced up to Octavia, waiting for their next instructions.

"Jon, you're good with machinery. Go to the mayor's comm station and keep trying to reach our missing families until you've raised someone. Wes, you have good eyes. I want you up in the observation turret. Kiernan and Gregor, go find all the people who brought their robo-harvesters into the village and fix any boulder-blasters and flame throwers that aren't functioning properly. Make sure that at least one of our big farm machines is stationed on each of the main streets just inside the eight gates to the village."

The young men ran off on their separate errands. Cyn McCarthy returned to report in, addressing both the mayor and Octavia at once. "The fence around Free Haven is reinforced, but they're still using several of the robo-harvesters to dig a trench around the perimeter."

Mayor Nikolai gave a grim nod. "Good thing I was able to talk the colonists into being prepared. Yes indeed."

Octavia and Cyn exchanged a look, but before Octavia could reply, Wes gave a shout from the observation turret. "Here they come! Aliens! You'd better get up here and see this for yourself."

Mayor Nikolai, Cyn, and Octavia ran to the turret and climbed the metal-runged ladder to the lookout tower. With dawn just beginning to break over the horizon, they were able to get a good look at the approaching menace.

No more than two kilometers away, a wave of creatures marched, scrambled, skittered, and loped toward the village.

The mayor swallowed convulsively.

"It's . . . it's an army," Cyn whispered in horror.

Hard, glossy carapaces provided armor for some of the creatures. Smaller ones raced forward like lizards with red eyes, lashing long tails. Some flew in the air, spreading wide leathery wings like dragons. Every type seemed to have more claws and teeth than any reasonable living creature needed to survive.

These monsters had been bred for only one thing.

As daylight brightened, the settlers could see that a good score of the shapes approaching them were distinctly human—or once had been. The colonists were infested by the creatures, just like Rastin. They all sported extra limbs, tentacles, eyes.

Sick at heart, Octavia said, "I think we know what happened to our missing families."

In stunned horror, Mayor Nikolai watched the relentless army approach. "There must be thousands of those things out there. How can we fight against that?"

Octavia gritted her teeth. "I don't think we have any choice."

CHAPTER 22

WHEN GENERAL DUKE'S BATTLECRUISERS PLOWED into the space battle in orbit, it reminded him of an expert break in a game of billiards.

Protoss craft and zerg minions scattered in all directions, reeling from the sudden strike of the unexpected terran forces. General Duke broadcast no warnings and requested no surrenders, just ordered his marines to inflict all the damage possible on the aliens.

He let out a loud whoop as the first shots were fired. The Yamato guns blasted quickly, taking out zerg overlords and one of the damaged carriers. Before the big energy weapons could recharge, General Duke launched his full fleet of impressively maneuverable wraiths.

He paced the bridge of his flagship, keeping an eye on the tactical displays, getting updates from Lieutenant Scott and occasionally watching the battle through the viewport windows.

"Have you ever seen so many explosions in your life, Lieutenant? Witnessed so much carnage?" Actually, Duke knew that Scott and the rest of Alpha Squadron had seen the dark and dirty side of war during their battles against the zerg in the defense of Mar Sara. But that didn't diminish his exhilaration one bit.

He turned to the comm officer. "Contact the settlers down there. We need a tactical update from the surface. I can't imagine how it can be any worse in the colony town than it is up here, but I need to set my military priorities."

"Yes, General." The comm officer bent over his station and tried to open a channel to the colonists on Bhekar Ro.

The wraiths launched from the terran fleet immediately cloaked before engaging a harried group of visible protoss scouts. The alien ships had superior air-to-air firepower, as Alpha Squadron knew from previous engagements in the recently ended war, but the scouts were obviously at a disadvantage against an adversary they could not see.

The wraiths pounded them, damaging their shields and hulls, taking out a handful of the vessels with their Gemini missiles. After heavy pummeling from the terran weapons, the protoss scouts retreated, inadvertently passing close to a mass of dragonlike mutalisks that completed the slaughter with an attack move that Duke's earlier briefings had called a "glave wurm," expelling waves of symbiotes that chewed and sliced their way through any hull they touched. The protoss scouts were doomed.

Their work done, the wraiths streaked off to engage more alien targets.

From the bridge of the *Norad III*, General Duke raised his fist with a shout, cheering the victory. The bridge officers applauded.

"Our Yamato gun is recharged and ready to fire, sir," Lieutenant Scott said. He tapped a voice receiver in his ear and acknowledged, then turned to look at the general. "Battlecruiser *Napoleon* also says their Yamato is ready to fire again."

"Good. Let's both target the same carrier," the general said. He stared at the broad selection of targets on the tactical screen. Dancing his fingers through the air, he muttered, "Eenie, Meenie, Minee, Mo," and jabbed his index finger forward. *"That* one."

"Targeting, sir," Lieutenant Scott said. He opened a link to the *Napoleon.* On cue, both terran warships fired their powerful guns, intense magnetic fields focusing a small nuclear explosion into a cohesive beam of energy. The concentrated onslaught hammered through the protoss shields. Within seconds, the carrier's hull failed and the giant alien vessel exploded.

General Duke let out another victorious hoot. "Who'd have thought those things could come in so many different pieces!" Next he watched the wraiths take out four more protoss scouts. He rubbed his stubby hands together and looked around at his bridge crew. "I think we can pretty much rest assured of a victory here, men."

Lieutenant Scott frowned. "Perhaps that would be a bit premature, General."

Two arbiters moved toward General Duke's fifteen clustered battlecruisers. Duke looked at them with a sneer. "And just what do they think they're doing? Move the fleet forward. Take the *Napoleon* and the *Bismarck* closer with a squad of eight wraiths to mop up the mess."

But as the two battlecruisers separated from the rest of Alpha Squadron, the darkness of space suddenly wavered. The arbiter fired a stasis field, an unfolding energy blanket that captured both battlecruisers along with three of the wraiths. Although the *Napoleon* and the *Bismarck* couldn't be attacked while seized by the stasis field, neither could they make any moves of their own.

With the stasis field in place, the five protoss carriers and eight scouts—all of which had been cloaked by the arbiter—moved forward to attack the now-exposed wraiths like angry hornets pouring out of a nest that a foolish child had beaten with a stick.

The wraith pilots attempted to cloak, but remained vulnerable when an observer exposed them again, stripping away their invisibility. The human pilots had no choice but to fire all their Gemini missiles in a last-ditch attempt to drive off the alien attackers, but streaking interceptors defended their ships. Without mercy, the alien fleet destroyed the five wraiths and moved into position, ready to open fire again as soon as the stasis field wore off . . .

The commanders of the *Napoleon* and the *Bismarck* howled at the treachery and launched their weapons. Once the stasis field was gone, forty more robotic interceptors spilled out of the uncloaked carriers and hammered like shotgun pellets into the two separated battlecruisers. The interceptors would normally have been little more than a nuisance, but in such a concentration they managed to inflict heavy damage.

Then, before General Duke could come to the defense of his ships, the zerg attacked Alpha Squadron's flank without so much as letting up in their offensive against the protoss. Flying through space, the hideous living creatures struck the terran ships.

Additional squadrons of wraiths rallied around General Duke's ships, trying to change their tactics to deal with the new threat, but the flying mutalisks launched repeated, insidious glave wurm strikes. A glave wurm struck one wraith, ripping into the systems, then ricocheted off to another single-man fighter, causing primary and collateral damage.

The squadron commander of the wraiths responded immediately by cloaking. After the ships vanished, they were able to turn the tide of the strike and return fire against the mutalisks. A zerg queen and swarms of smaller self-destructive scourges detached from the main battle against the protoss and spread through space, searching for the rest of the cloaked wraith squadron.

Duke was proud to see his own small fighters continue to blast the zerg scum out of space, wreaking terrible damage. The dark vacuum was filled with broken carapaces and flash-frozen alien slime.

"Sir, the zerg overlords are catching up with us," Lieutenant Scott said. "We know they can breach our cloaking fields. They'll expose all of our wraiths. Should we withdraw them now?"

General Duke scowled. "Not on your life, Lieutenant. Just look at the damage we're doing to the enemy."

Meanwhile, the barrage of interceptors had managed to cripple the *Bismarck,* and the battlecruiser *Napoleon* could not find enough power to retreat to safety. When the overlords drew close to the unseen wraith squadron, they exposed the swift terran fighters so that a queen could close in and choose her target. Thrashing herself into position, she launched a wide, rapidly spreading web of greenish goo. The thick resin splashed into the ion intakes of the fast fighters, dramatically slowing the wraiths' controls, overloading their detectors, and clogging their weapons. Dragonlike mutalisks attacked with even more frenzy than before.

Then the hordes of small but suicidal scourge's slammed into them. The tiny zerg beasts were like living cannonballs, thinking bombs that chose their targets and crashed against hulls, exploding and wiping out wraith after wraith.

"General!" Lieutenant Scott shouted, and Duke

could no longer deny that he needed to reassess the situation.

"Pull back the fleet!" he said. "We need to regroup."

Anticipating the command—or perhaps praying for it—Lieutenant Scott sent out the order before the general finished speaking. No crew member aboard would dare comment on General Duke's overconfidence, though they all must have been thinking the same thing.

With the *Bismarck* dead in space and the *Napoleon* trying to limp back under continued attack, General Duke drew together what remained of Alpha Squadron. "Send a science vessel to scan the main cluster of protoss ships. I want to know how many more are out there hiding like spiders in a woodpile."

As two science vessels glided forward, they employed their signature weapon, an electromagnetic pulse that rippled across space and washed over the battlefield like a tidal wave. The EMP removed the energy shielding from all the protoss ships, leaving them vulnerable—if not to the weapons of Alpha Squadron, then at least to the zerg.

General Duke swallowed hard and concentrated on covering his own ass, since his flagship was taking a pounding. "I want another science vessel to deploy a defensive matrix over the *Norad III*. Keep us safe!" He quickly realized his verbal blunder. "Uh, and the matrix should cover any other battlecruiser within range, of course. We need to protect our men. All of them. We've got to stay alive even if it means retreat," he said, though the words caught in his throat like a chunk of rotten lemon.

He fumed as he stared at the tactical screen, realizing that his forces might be in for a tougher fight than he had counted on.

CHAPTER 23

THE COLONISTS' DESPERATE PREPARATIONS WERE completed none too soon. The alien monsters attacked at dawn.

Octavia stood inside the fence near the steel-walled prefabricated buildings at the perimeter of Free Haven. She was exhausted. Her eyes felt scratchy. She had not slept for two days, but could not imagine resting right now.

They might all be dead in a few hours.

A robo-harvester blocked each gateway to the village. Two of the rock-crushing mining machines could be put into service as makeshift tanks, if the situation got desperate enough.

Once she got a look at the approaching zerg in the first rays of sunlight, heard the humming, clacking rumble of the hordes, and saw the clouds of dust they churned up while marching across the flattened agricultural plains, Octavia knew that their situation had become desperate indeed.

Next to her, Mayor Nikolai took a step back in astonishment. "My God."

The settlers had distributed their stockpile of home-grown weapons, small projectile launchers, pulse pistols, and rarely used hunting guns. Some of them gripped farm implements—large scythes and sharp-ended weeding tools. A farmer with tough muscles could use them as effectively as any warrior used a spear.

Gasping, the other colonists gripped their weapons as if they were lifelines. Although Octavia herself had sounded the warning about the aliens, the menace of this swarm was orders of magnitude more powerful than she had imagined. The monstrous creatures seemed limitless.

"The perimeter fences are our first line of defense!" she shouted. None of the settlers had military experience, but she knew they had to stop the first wave, or all would be lost. "We have to keep them from getting into the town. Don't hold back on your weapons. If our lines break and we scatter, we'll each end up fighting by ourselves. They'll pick us off one by one."

Ignoring her, two of the settlers bolted for the dubious shelter of their homes.

"Stand and fight!" Octavia yelled to the rest.

Mayor Nikolai muttered something about needing to check on the children, but Octavia grabbed his arm and held him in place.

The first scout ranks of aliens, low runners with sharp razor-limb sickles, reached the perimeter of the settlement. About the size of a dog, the aliens looked like big lizards with red eyes, sharp claws, and multiple rending arms. In a massive wave, they raced across the dirt with a pattering thunder like giant hungry crabs.

The colonists' first shots rang out, many of them going wild because the weapons were poorly aimed. But because of the sheer number of alien scouts, most of the shots struck *something*. The other scout aliens stampeded over their fallen companions, either ripping them to shreds with razor-limbs or ignoring them in their death throes. It looked like an unending wave of hideous death.

Octavia felt despair overwhelm her terror. What chance did they possibly have? She had brought a pellet blaster from home, which she fired again and again. At first she took a grim pride in watching the creatures she slaughtered, but then there was no time even to pay attention. She blazed out pellets until she exhausted her stockpile of ammunition. Many of the other colonists had also run dry of shotpacks for their projectile weapons or battery cartridges for their pulse pistols.

The first mob of small aliens attacked, breaking through the fence line and raising their scythe-claws to slash and tear. Colonists screamed. Octavia watched several people fall in bloody piles of dismantled flesh. And it was just the beginning.

Kiernan and Kirsten Warner—he a young stonemason, she a teacher and amateur engineer—fought side by side with the granite-chopping implements Kiernan used in his work. He swung the long tool from one side to the other, hacking sharp limbs off the creatures, splitting their thick leathery hides, and leaving a pile of twitching, mindless alien bodies around him. Kirsten fought just as hard, as if trying to keep up with the number of victims Kiernan scattered on the ground.

Mayor Nikolai turned and bolted. Octavia shouted for him to come back, but like a true politician, he had an excuse for his hasty retreat. "I need to send an urgent call to the terran fleet! They should have arrived by now. I've got to tell them what's going on down here." Without waiting, Nikolai ran and barricaded himself inside the communications turret.

Octavia didn't have time to worry about it. She hurled her empty, useless pellet gun at the closest lizardlike alien with such force that it smashed open the thing's head. Ooze splattered, but that didn't seem to bother the creature a bit.

As she stood for a fraction of a second, weaponless, Octavia remembered the old missile turret, the decorative monument that had surprised them all by activating itself and shooting the observer out of the skies. Even with its automated systems burned out, the turret still had a few intact missiles. There should be enough explosives to cause some damage.

The missile turret was made for shooting at airborne targets, but it no longer functioned as it had been designed to do. Perhaps she could launch the rockets manually.

Octavia needed only one minute. It was all the time she had.

She raced for the center of town, a place that had once been peaceful, the closest thing to a park on Bhekar Ro. Behind her, the terrified colonists were forced to fall back, their lines crumbling as the blood-thirsty alien hordes attacked them. The makeshift weapons were beginning to falter, but Octavia concentrated only on the large piece of equipment.

Although she and Jon had managed to fix the mechanical parts of the gun, the electronics were completely unsalvageable. But these comprised mostly the sensors and the automated targeting systems, Octavia realized. She climbed up the metal-runged ladder and ripped open the access panel.

All she needed were the firing controls.

Using her legs and shoulder, she pushed upward, swinging the missile launcher down and swiveling it with brute force toward the oncoming alien troops. She had only two missiles left and didn't know exactly how much damage each one would cause.

Finding the trigger controls, she did her best to eye-ball a trajectory, pointing the first of the small surface-to-air missiles at the center of the slavering monsters. It would be good to watch them blow up.

Squeezing one eye shut, whispering a quick prayer, she launched the first weapon. The explosive-filled projectile roared through the air, whistling and spinning. At first she thought her shot would miss, but then she saw it plow down into a cluster of the alien scouts. Flashes of fire and smoke and broken monstrous parts flew in all directions, sending the attacking creatures spinning like a hive of maddened ants.

In the moment of stunned surprise, Octavia saw no point in waiting. She swung the missile turret slightly to the left, where the lizardlike alien creatures were regrouping, then launched her second—and last— missile. She watched the new explosion with exhilaration. She had single-handedly wiped out hundreds of the attackers!

Unfortunately, the ravenous invading forces had many hundreds to spare.

As the dust and smoke settled, a brief silence hovered for a few seconds over the battlefield. Several colonists cheered at this. Others screamed in pain. The swarm of deadly aliens gathered themselves again, making hissing and buzzing noises.

Then Octavia saw what she feared most shambling out of the carnage—hulking forms, slightly man-shaped, yet twisted and distorted. The bodies had once been human. The farmers had been strong; the women had been beautiful in a coarse sort of way. But now these infested settlers had been taken over completely by the controlling alien invaders.

They plodded forward, a mass of tentacles, slashing claws, and hideous stingers that dripped venom. They looked as if a mad dollmaker had grafted extra parts onto what had previously been perfectly normal human forms.

Several of the front-line defenders wailed as the infested colonists came forward. "It's Gandhi, and Liberty Ryan! And there's Brutus Jensen."

Octavia recognized these people with a twist of revulsion. The settlers had been her neighbors. They had all worked hard to plant seedlings, protecting and nurturing them out in the agricultural fields. Brutus Jensen had been a hardworking farm hand.

The infested colonists walked forward. Free Haven's defenders were uneasy, reluctant to fire upon people who until today had been their friends.

But now they were all monsters. Enemies. Just like the prospector Rastin.

When Octavia saw their skin begin to squirm, their bodies boil, their faces and stomachs swell and puff, she remembered what had happened to Old Blue—a buildup of toxic and explosive gases. "Get away from them!" she shouted, running toward the perimeter. "Don't let them come closer!"

But she was too far away. Some of the colonists heard her and turned to look, while others were too frozen with horror to listen.

Octavia threw herself to the ground, flinching instinctively as the infested colonists came as close as they could manage before their bodies exploded like biological bombs filled with poisonous vapors and chemicals.

The violent eruption of the Ryans and poor young

Brutus Jensen knocked out the front line of the Bhekar Ro defenders. Three colonists were killed instantly. Thirty meters of fence and two entire perimeter buildings were knocked over by the shock wave. Other defenders who had stood too close fell rolling on the ground, gasping and choking, coughing blood as the poison worked its way through their systems in a quick but agonizing death.

Many alien scouts in the vicinity were also wiped out, but Octavia had seen by now that the invading forces considered each individual creature to be completely expendable.

She got to her feet and saw a new wave of monsters approaching, then glanced over to the sealed doors of the comm turret where Mayor Nikolai had barricaded himself. She hoped he'd been able to contact the terran fleet.

If the military "rescuers" did not get down here soon, there wouldn't be any colonists left to rescue.

CHAPTER 24

IN THE PROTOSS BASE CAMP IN THE SHADOW OF the magnificent xel'naga artifact, Executor Koronis stood beside the curved wing of the large arbiter. With a flurry of telepathic signals, he tried to follow the complex battle among the enemy forces in orbit. He remained in contact with Templar Mess'Ta aboard his flagship, receiving tactical updates.

Koronis spoke through the all-fleet telepathic channel, knowing that none of their enemies could hear or understand the powerful mental transmission. "Show no mercy against the enemies of the First Born. You must protect this great prize for the protoss race. Our success here will decide whether the *Qel'Ha* returns to Aiur in triumph, or as a thrice-beaten failure."

Mess'Ta responded, "We all know what is at stake, Executor. We will not falter. Our resolve will never weaken."

Koronis signed off, knowing he could not have left

the *Qel'Ha* in better hands, unless he himself was in orbit. But he had another job to do here.

Flanked by four other judicators, Judicator Amdor stood below the object, raising his hands high and spreading his claws. They all clustered together, mentally chanting, sensing the vibrations from the Khala as they attempted to detect nuances from the glowing object.

Koronis stepped up to them, watching. Before being promoted to executor, he had been a High Templar himself, proficient in many telepathic abilities. He could feel the emanations from the exposed object, but could not determine the origin, could not comprehend whether it was a message or a warning.

Amdor turned to the executor and indicated the silvery clear spines of large crystal growths that rose like broken snowflakes from the rubble of the avalanche. "Look at the Khaydarin crystals! These alone are enough wealth to make the entire Conclave rejoice."

"Those crystals, Judicator, are a mark of the Xel'Naga. Their very presence proves that this object is far more valuable than we had at first dreamed."

Amdor fairly glowed with satisfaction and pleasure. "We must explore, Executor. Let us go inside with all possible haste."

Koronis had made other plans, though. "I have ordered a group of dragoons to prepare."

Amdor looked frustrated, but bowed his gray head. Despite his personal ambitions, the judicator could not argue with such a wise precaution.

Koronis turned and sent a signal to the nearest arbiter. The wings of the big ship opened. With ponderous clanking movements that grew smoother as the cyborg warriors exercised and proceeded forward, four dragoons came down the ramp.

Encased in a spherical body core and propelled by four large spiderlike legs, the dragoons plodded along. These were veteran protoss warriors who had been crippled or mortally wounded in combat. Rather than dying in service of the Khala, they had chosen to have their bodily remnants transplanted into these mechanical exoskeletons.

The walkers lumbered forward in their armored bodies. The brains of the shattered volunteers focused energies through the Khala in order to control the movements of dragoon limbs. Their articulated legs were able to scramble over the rough terrain and climb the broken rock wall more easily than the robed judicators ever could.

During the *Qel'Ha*'s long and fruitless search, these dragoons had waited, unused, fearing they would never contribute to the overall mission. Their greatest concern was that their sacrifice in becoming these living mechanical walkers would be in vain.

Now the dragoons had a purpose.

The first protoss explorers to enter the exposed xel'naga artifact clambered upward until they reached the opening tunnels. Koronis and Amdor stood together and watched as the brave dragoons entered the mysterious labyrinth.

CHAPTER 25

THE BATTLE FOR FREE HAVEN CONTINUED WITH-
out any glimmer of hope for the struggling settlers.
Octavia had no time to plan ahead or worry about the
future—only to survive for the moment, and kill as
many zerg as possible.

But the ravenous alien invaders did not need to
rest.

Some of the settlers fought hand to hand, using
farm implements in a desperate attempt to stem the
tide of monstrous creatures. Octavia had no more
missiles to fire and no hand weapon. She raced
toward the nearest robo-harvester, a big lumbering
vehicle that Mayor Nikolai kept for his own use. She
knew the man did not maintain it as well as she and
Lars had kept their own vehicle, which now lay dead
near the site of the alien artifact. But the robo-harvester
could still cause a lot of damage.

She bounded up the treads, stepped on the metal
running board, threw herself inside the huge vehicle,

and powered up the engines. A snort of vespene exhaust coughed out of the top stack like smoke from a dragon's nostril.

Across the town plaza, which now became a hunting ground for the zerglings that had broken through the settlers' first defenses, she watched the stonemason Kiernan Warner and his wife Kirsten jump into one of the ponderous, slow-moving mining machines. They sealed themselves into the armored vehicle and began to plow forward.

Octavia found the harvester controls, knocked aside some clutter and trinkets the mayor had left in the driver's seat, and surged ahead, treads clanking through the streets. Clenching her teeth tightly together, she pushed the giant vehicle forward, ready to meet the next wave of zerg. Behind the small stampeding attackers she saw bigger monsters, including nine of the hunched serpentine creatures that had shot needle spines at her as she fled in the little field crawler from Rastin's homestead. *Hydralisks.*

The monsters' fang-filled jaws opened all the way back to their stunted leather ears, and black soulless eyes stared at her as the creatures reared up in defiance of this mechanical foe.

Before she even moved close enough to fire a boulder blaster, the first hydralisk bent its hunched, hard back and launched a volley of needle projectiles. She heard them spang and ricochet off the thick walls of the robo-harvester. Octavia flinched as one bounced against the windshield, leaving a snowflake of damaged glass. She pushed the growling engines to their limits and bore down upon the first zerg monster as it prepared to fire again.

The creature was powerful and armed with more of the needle projectiles, but it was no match for the mass and momentum of the giant harvesting machine. It flailed its clawed arms, trying to grasp the robo-harvester and wrestle it to the ground, but she rolled over the thing with her heavy treads, squashing it into a puddle of crunched exoskeleton and spreading goo.

Next, two of the remaining hydralisks converged on her from opposite sides, each hammering the vehicle with another volley of spines. She heard the pattering clang as the projectiles crashed into the metal walls, scratching and denting the hull. A few poked all the way through, leaving bright air holes, but Octavia did not cringe.

Instead, she activated the powerful combine arm, a huge rolling basket with sharpened blades that could mow down fields of triticale-wheat. She lowered the combine arm like a blurring flyswatter onto one of the spine-depleted hydralisks. The monster flailed and thrashed even as it was chopped into a thousand pieces. Slime and blood splattered her machine's windshield.

Dizzy with her success, Octavia swung the combine arm to the left and bore down on the third hydralisk, which lurched backward as if suddenly sensing its danger. She plowed over that one as well, then careened forward as three more monsters clustered in a concerted effort to stop her.

Octavia squeezed her eyes shut and drove ahead. She didn't know if the whirring blades of the harvesting arm or the crushing treads themselves destroyed the new batch of hydralisks—but when the robo-harvester clanked past, she saw that she had left all of them dead, their few intact limbs and body parts still twitching on the crushed ground.

Kiernan Warner had brought his mining machine close enough to dig into the rocky ground at the edge of the battered perimeter fence. The boulder catapult seized hard stones and began to launch them like cannonballs into the zerg forces.

Dozens of frantic zerglings were pulverized into bloody spray. The rock thrower struck two more hydralisks, punching boulders through their hard carapaces. In its death throes, one of the ferocious creatures sprayed a cloud of poison needles in all directions. Some of them struck the cumbersome mining machine, others flew like wild arrows into the sky, while the remainder of the spines slaughtered other enemy aliens that surged forward into the gap.

Stunned by the sudden turnabout and vehemence of the colonists' defense, the attacking forces hesitated. Octavia saw the creatures fall back, their numbers vastly diminished.

But soon the zerg circled around the octagonal perimeter of Free Haven and approached from the northeast, where they massed, ready for a full-fledged invasion of the town.

"They're trying to break through to the fuel depot!" she muttered to herself, looking toward the industrial area where the colonists stored their tanks of refined vespene gas.

Free Haven always kept a fuel stockpile "for emergencies," Mayor Nikolai said, although Octavia was half convinced that the settlers had maintained such a large reservoir of volatile vespene so that they didn't often need to deal with the grouchy old recluse Rastin.

She felt a pang of sadness, knowing that the prospector had been one of the first casualties of the zerg swarm. Well, now maybe his painstakingly harvested vespene could help with the defense of Bhekar Ro.

Octavia used the robo-harvester's front flamethrower to blast out a column of fire that withered the nearby zerglings. The built-in flamethrower had originally been designed for clear-cutting dense forests to make way for new arable land. Now she used it to cremate a field of enemies.

One of the hydralisks turned defiantly to face her, rising up tall and hissing, but she incinerated it with a fireball right in its ugly face.

The treads of the robo-harvester clanked over the uneven ground as she made her way toward the fuel depot. Perhaps the alien army sensed this was a weak point in the town's defenses, or maybe they just wanted the vespene for themselves. The monsters clustered near the depot and moved forward together.

The zerg passed through the town's weakened fences as if they were no more than thin strings, and piled into the open area of vespene storage tanks.

Octavia knew she would only have a few seconds, and she had to act now or her wild plan was doomed. She locked down the robo-harvester's treads and let loose with the full long-range stream of her flamethrower, trying to blanket the fuel depot. Dozens of the zerglings shriveled and crisped. Two hydralisks moved through the diluted flames, singeing their glossy hides, though the creatures did not appear to notice any pain.

Octavia's target, however, was not the hideous monstrosities.

After a few agonized seconds during which she doubted the heat would be sufficient, the first and nearest storage tank reached its critical temperature. The vespene fuel erupted in a fireball that knocked out the next tank, setting it on fire, which in turn blew up the third, like a game of incandescent dominoes.

The enormous blast rippled outward, flash-crisping all the zerg forces within the fuel depot, knocking flat any others on the periphery. The explosion continued to build, and Octavia held on to her seat as the robo-harvester bucked and rolled.

When the smoke and flames cleared, she saw to her amazement that the bulk of the attacking swarm had been annihilated through the fiery explosions, as well as the other colonists' continued efforts.

The remaining zerg troops on the fringe backed off, either from fear or a sense of defeat.

Dazed, Octavia climbed out of the robo-harvester. The surviving colonists emerged from their hiding places, some of them pale with shock, others drenched with blood—both red blood and inhuman greenish ichor.

Kiernan and Kirsten stumbled out of their mining machine, mouths open, looking amazed. No one seemed to believe the skirmish had been won, that they had driven off the implacable invading aliens.

Mayor Nikolai emerged from the shelter of his comm turret, grinning as triumphantly as a conquering hero. "I've done it! Good news. I've contacted the terran forces. The military will be here soon."

Some of the settlers groaned, others cheered. Octavia felt too numb to complain about the mayor's actions. She slumped against the dirty treads of the robo-harvester, heaved several exhausted breaths, then looked up in awe as she heard a new rumbling, hissing sound, much louder than the one they had heard at dawn.

The third and largest wave of zerg marched across the plains—not just small scout creatures and a few hydralisks this time, but gigantic monsters as well, like nightmarish versions of prehistoric woolly mammoths with enormous scythelike tusks that looked capable of slicing buildings in half.

In the skies, a cluster of twisted dragonlike creatures swept along the winds, heading toward the settlement. Dozens and dozens of hydralisks slithered along in the front row. They kept coming. In addition, Octavia saw many other minions, twisted breeds, horrifying mutations, all of them looking deadly, all of them intent on wiping out the terran settlers.

Octavia could only stare in defeat. This wave would be unstoppable.

CHAPTER 26

IN ORBIT OVER BHEKAR RO, THE SHIPS OF ALPHA Squadron continued to be battered and pounded by the frenzied protoss and zerg space fleets.

General Edmund Duke paced the control bridge. "Well, men, it sounds as if we need to leave this little playground behind," he said, looking at the message his comm officer had given him. "Those colonists need our help, so we'll have to go down to the surface and take care of that firestorm right away."

Lieutenant Scott watched the flaming hulk that remained of the *Bismarck* and saw the damaged battlecruiser *Napoleon* limping along, trying to break free of the converging alien forces. "Is that tactically wise, General? Our forces are in dire straits up here."

Frowning, Duke turned his craggy face toward the tactical officer. "Lieutenant Scott, it would be quite an embarrassment if we came all this way to rescue colonists, and then let the aliens gobble them up before we could help." He had learned long ago that becoming a war hero was due as much to public relations as it was to tactical brilliance. "Don't worry. We'll leave some ships in place, though, so they can keep fighting the enemy."

The lieutenant gave combat orders, directing the main force of terran battle vessels to break off their orbital conflict and descend to the surface. To the rest of the human ships left in space to defend against the zerg and protoss, it looked as if they were running away.

"This is not a retreat," General Duke insisted. "We are initiating an offensive in the opposite direction."

The vanguard of Alpha Squadron plunged through the dusty skies like a cavalry riding in to save the besieged terrans of Free Haven. Below, Duke could see the town smoldering. A great deal of damage had already been done. But the colonists had survived so far.

The general saw the stampede of zerg sweeping across the flat ground to surround and engulf the octagonal settlement. Some of the enemy creatures had already broken through the fence, but at the sight of the numerous alien bodies strewn around—not to mention the smoking craters and the flaming debris—General Duke was impressed that the settlers had been able to mount such an effective resistance, for a bunch of clodhoppers.

Now all he needed to do was save enough of them so he could show clips of his success on the Universal News Network. He smiled. "Alien scum." He ordered his ships to fire.

Alpha Squadron entered the dirtside fray like a bull in a china shop, striking at anything that moved, though making an effort to avoid anything that appeared human. Ranks of airborne zerg—a subspecies that General Duke recognized as mutalisks—flew upward, spitting green acid slime through the air. For some reason, though, the mutalisks did not engage the battlecruisers. Instead, the flying monsters pulled away, ascending toward the orbital conflict. They had probably been summoned by the overlords in space to engage the protoss forces, now that the terran military had broken off from that particular fight.

That was fine with General Duke.

Terran dropships swooped low to the ground and delivered Arclite siege tanks, heavily shielded soldiers wearing combat armor, and scavenger hover bikes called vultures. These military units advanced, prepared to engage any creatures on the ground.

The general made no attempt to reestablish contact with the political administration in the terran colony. This was a military operation, and he would damn well do what he felt was necessary.

His men knew the drill. They spread out to build defensive perimeters while the small wraiths and huge battlecruisers provided air support against the advancing zerg. Using full firepower, the Alpha Squadron ships struck repeatedly, pounding even the mammoth-sized ultralisks, wiping out waves of the remaining zerglings, crushing groups of hydralisks.

"This is more like it," Duke said, and took over some of the firing controls for himself just to keep in practice.

With the flying, acid-spitting mutalisks gone and no enemy air attack imminent, Duke's assault became a one-sided rout. After hours of absolute slaughter, he ended up losing only eleven wraiths, five goliaths, and a handful of marines and firebats, all of whom would get honorable citations signed by Emperor Arcturus Mengsk himself—if the Dominion had new stationery printed yet.

As the *Norad III* landed outside the smoking town, General Duke disembarked with his shoulders squared, his chin held high. He expected cheers, though the surviving rescued settlers looked exhausted and stunned.

Frowning slightly, he saw that his marines and firebats had caused about as much destruction to the town buildings as the zerg had. Unfortunate. Still, it was friendly fire, so the colonists shouldn't complain. "Collateral damage, that's all," he muttered to himself as he marched down the street of his newly conquered town.

He looked for the mayor or, if the zerg had killed the man, somebody else who could formally turn over control to this military operation. He looked around at the colonists, imagining that they viewed him as their savior.

"I'll make this my ground base of operations now," he said as more marines emerged from a just-landed dropship. He debated whether to make a speech first or to order his marines to help extinguish some of the fires in the town. In a gracious gesture, he dispatched battlefield medics to see if they could help any of the wounded settlers.

He smiled proudly and turned to the bedraggled colonists. "You civilians can all rest easy now."

CHAPTER 27

OUT AT THE SITE OF OLD RASTIN'S HOMESTEAD, the prospector's shack and refinery structures had *evolved*. They were now completely covered with living organic matter.

Hard exoskeletons grew up in tangled, twisted labyrinths following the genetic model of a zerg hive, a pattern that no human could comprehend. The fleshy biomass of zerg creep continued to spread, absorbing raw materials from the rough dirt and processing it into a nourishing substance.

While many queens had landed with the arrival of Kukulkan Brood, this one had remained in the hatchery established at Rastin's homestead. The only purpose of this place was to spawn larvae by the hundreds, each of which would evolve into one of the various minions.

Ducking her triangular head on a long, sinuous neck, the queen raised her pointed arms. She knew her part in the mission. Sarah Kerrigan, the new Queen of Blades, had planted full instructions in the minds of the Kukulkan overlords, which controlled all the queens and their hatcheries. The queen, in turn, controlled all the wasplike drones that moved about building the hatchery, grasping material with their clacking claws. They evolved the hatchery through the intermediary stage of a defensible lair until, finally, this conquered outpost would become a full-fledged zerg hive.

Kukulkan Brood had a variety of minions to meet any resistance. Like giant insects, drones went about their work, following instructions, utterly loyal. The larvae continued to mutate from spiny grubs into zerglings, hydralisks, even mammoth ultralisks. Newborn mutalisks took to the skies, ready to launch aerial attacks with hurled acid.

And there was something new. The queen, following her zerg instincts, had absorbed the DNA of the large blue-furred dog that had been infested here. The zerg considered the ferocious animal a potential candidate for an experimental new strain of minion.

Throughout their race's history, the zerg had conquered other species and acquired superior traits from their genetics. When the swarm had first attacked the old prospector and his dog, the queen had seen genetic characteristics and capabilities the zerg did not have—yet.

Though Old Blue had already succumbed to the initial infestation, the queen had catalogued and remembered the canine DNA. As an experiment, she began to incorporate the improvements in the dog's musculature—and, most important, an advanced sense of smell—into new larvae. In several test creatures, the queen designed fearsome zerg traits into large mastiff bodies that resembled the blue-furred dog . . .

Under the old refinery structure, her drones burrowed deep beneath the ground, moving buried boulders in crustal shafts to reawaken all four of the vespene geysers. Then a drone metamorphosed into a living Extractor over the spouts of valuable energetic gas. The Extractor collected the outpouring vespene and packaged it in concentrated fleshy sacks, which were brought back to the hatchery. Some of the gas was used to create other zerg minions for the conquering force. Some was sent to zerg soldiers, which consumed the substance, drawing power and nourishment to continue the fight against their enemies.

The newborn minions tunneled into the ground or spread across the surface, expanding outward in an unstoppable force. While the attack on the colony town had been a serious effort, it was only a small part of the overall strategy of Kukulkan Brood.

The human colonists were potential resources, but they were also life-forms that could offer resistance to the zerg plan. Ultimately, though, the settlers were irrelevant.

The main zerg objective was elsewhere, across the ridge and in the next valley, where protoss forces had already landed . . .

*   *   *

Walking like mechanical spiders driven by living brains, the protoss dragoons had disappeared into the cathedral shape of the xel'naga artifact.

But before Executor Koronis could receive a report on their explorations, his ground troops of fanatical zealots sounded an alarm. They reeled backward as the valley surface began to ripple and crack.

Then a storm of zerg attackers emerged from the ground, boiling up from hidden burrows. Hydralisks heaved upward, their curved backs bent forward so that their volleys of poisonous needle spines sliced the closest protoss soldiers to ribbons.

Koronis's zealots screamed and rushed forward into the fray. Though they had not yet reached the highest levels of the Khala, the templar warriors were ruthless and fanatically dedicated to defending their race. Enhanced with cybernetic grafts, the zealots wore sophisticated power suits complete with curved shoulder crests, breastplates, and padded greaves. On their thick forearm units they wore enhancements to channel their psionic energy, focusing it into a deadly psionic blade. The zealots charged into battle with full fury, slashing with shimmering psionic blades to mow down the alien attackers.

Reacting to the sudden zerg offensive, Executor Koronis summoned his ground forces, calling out his High Templars and launching the sluggish but deadly reavers—armored units that looked like huge cater-pillars—and more of his mobile cyborg dragoons.

Following their leader's command without question, many zealots sacrificed themselves in order to draw the zerg together, concentrating them. Koronis saw his chance.

Standing on the rocky foothills beneath the huge pulsing artifact, the executor summoned up the energies inside him. He used one of his greatest weapons, learned from decades of studying the most subtle nuances of the Khala by meditating on his small fragment of crystal on board the *Qel'Ha*.

A psionic storm.

The giant Khaydarin crystals littered around the xel'naga artifact reflected his telepathic energy, focusing his attack so that the mental storm continued to build, gathering power.

From higher up, closer to the fringe of the once-buried artifact, Judicator Amdor looked down with concern and amazement. Crackling, energy-saturated wind blasted his dark robes until they flapped around him like angry flames. His eyes blazed.

Below, Koronis did not hold back. He released his psionic storm with the most terrible blast he had ever conjured. The roiling energy roared down at the concentrated zerg minions, and he felt a searing satisfaction when the blast incinerated dozens of the ferocious alien troops.

Weakened, the executor fell back as the wind and the light began to fade into the sky. But the struggle was not over.

Again, his zealots charged forward, their psionic blades ignited. The battle had just been joined. Koronis blinked with amazement to see other sections of the ground crack open, spewing forth even more zerg attackers.

He ordered his carriers to come down and form a solid fortification around the artifact—their prize. More help could not arrive quickly enough, as far as Koronis was concerned.

Right now he could see only more and more of the zerg rushing forward in an unstoppable wave . . .

CHAPTER 28

WHEN THE BLUSTERY AND DESTRUCTIVE TERRAN marines took over the town of Free Haven, Octavia Bren didn't see much of an improvement over the zerg invasion.

While the surviving settlers rushed to put out fires, tend to their wounded, and bury their dead, General Duke commandeered the largest intact building in front of the town square and then pulled out a folding command chair from his battlecruiser. He and his men moved with practiced military precision to set up their base camp inside the town limits.

While Abdel and Shayna Bradshaw took care of the injured colonists who had been carried to the meeting hall, Octavia saw to those who still lay where they had fallen. She moved from one bleeding neighbor to another, tending their cuts and broken bones with plastiscab bandages, flexsplints, and antibiotics, rapidly draining Free Haven's already small store of first-aid supplies.

Octavia looked around for help. Everyone was either wounded or occupied on urgent business—except for the terran military. Indignant, she strode up to where the self-satisfied general sat in his folding command chair in the town plaza, directing military operations.

"The colonists are dying," she announced. "We need medical supplies and personnel."

General Duke hardly glanced at her. "My men are busy. We've got to set up the base camp."

"Your men—and *you*, General—were sent here to *help* us." Octavia was not about to give up. People were dying. Her *friends* were dying. She locked her gaze with the general's, refusing to be ignored.

Finally he dispatched a dozen more of his cruiser's field medics to assist in the operations and had another medic fetch an entire crate of field hospital supplies. Octavia knew Duke did it more to get rid of her than out of humanitarian concerns. For now, though, all she cared about was results.

The marines of Alpha Squadron trundled down the battlecruisers' loading ramps with a dozen SCVs to gather vital minerals and stock up on vespene gas (since Octavia herself had been forced to obliterate the town's fuel depot).

Octavia splinted Jon's broken leg and moved on to a shocked twelve-year-old boy who had lost a lot of blood. She gave him an infusion of plasma and a potent pain reliever. Then she glanced up and watched with curiosity as a ruddy-faced Mayor Nikolai marched toward Duke, bony fists balled, scrawny arms bent as if for the first time in his life he could imagine punching someone.

"General, your men are gutting our buildings. They've stolen engines and supplies from our homes, and now you've sent them out on vehicles to raid our farm dwellings! We've survived the zerg only to be plundered by our so-called rescuers. How dare you! Explain yourself."

General Duke scowled. "You called for us to rescue you, Mayor. Alpha Squadron was in the midst of a difficult conflict in orbit, but we broke free, landed here, and saved your collective butts. I'd think you'd be a bit more grateful."

Mayor Nik spluttered. "Of course we're grateful. But if we die from the zerg today or die from starvation a month from now, we'll still all be dead."

"Now, now, Mayor. Before Alpha Squadron departs we can leave you some of our prepackaged Meals Ready-to-Eat. Why, I'm sure we've got a couple thousand thermal packs of Chipped Beef Deluxe that are close to their expiration dates."

Nik protested, but the general waved him away. "I assure you, we're only doing what is necessary to accomplish our objective. Alpha Squadron has its orders, you know. We've done our best to help you and these dirt farmers out, but I've got an enemy to defeat and an alien artifact to claim in the name of the emperor." He turned a baleful look on the mayor and scratched his stubbly jowl. "I warn you, don't interfere with my men, or I'll commandeer another one of your town buildings and use it as a brig."

Two marines hauled Mayor Nik away as he struggled and squirmed like a child being taken from a favorite toy.

Once the general had been debriefed by a handful of colonists his troops acquired at random, he sent marines to look specifically for Octavia Bren, who had sounded the original alarm and apparently had more close experience with the aliens than anyone else in Free Haven.

Without offering an explanation, he had her escorted to his new command center—formerly Mayor Nikolai's home—and sat back at his desk to assess her. He didn't offer her any refreshments. She felt a renewed dislike for him.

"Now, Miz Brown," he said in a gravelly voice.

"Bren, General. It's *Bren.*"

"Yes, of course, ma'am. Now, it's time for you to do your duty as a citizen of the Terran Dominion."

Octavia stood straight and gave him a small frown. "Here on Bhekar Ro we're independent, General. We'd never heard of your Dominion until we sent a message just a few days ago, so how could we be citizens of it?"

"Nevertheless, Emperor Mengsk loves and counts on all of his subjects—even the ignorant ones." He drummed his thick fingers on the desktop. "I understand that you, more than anyone else in the settlement, know about this mysterious alien artifact. You've seen it with your own eyes."

"It killed my brother, General."

"Good, good," he said. "Not about your brother, I mean, but that you've got up-close experience. Now, ma'am, tell me everything you remember. What does it look like? What are the defenses around it? What else did you observe about its potential as a *weapon*, perhaps? If this thing can help us conquer the enemy, then we can leave you and your fellow farmers in peace. Wouldn't you like to go back to doing . . . whatever it is you colonists do?"

Octavia wanted nothing more in the world, so she gave him the details. Starting with how she and her brother had found the object exposed after an avalanche, she explained how it had killed Lars and later fried her robo-harvester.

General Duke raised his eyebrows. "Interesting. Perhaps it could be adapted to putting enemy vehicles out of commission. Like a lockdown strike. Hmmm, I'll have a team of science specialists study it up close."

"I think all those aliens that arrived have the same idea," she said. "Your scientists may be in for a surprise."

"Don't worry your pretty little head, my girl. We've had experience with both the zerg and the protoss before." He looked around at various instruments he had rewired in the mayor's dwelling, including the seismographs taken from the Brens' own home.

Offhandedly, as if recounting his glory days, he gave her a bit of background about the first war between the protoss and the terrans and the zerg.

As Octavia listened to him brag, she looked over at the repaired seismographs and saw them jiggling, picking up numerous explosions, all of them centered around the artifact out in the distant valley. "It looks like there's a disturbance out there, General."

Duke quickly studied the blips and pursed his thick lips. "I can ascertain that these are weapons signatures. Must be the echoes of a big battle—and my men aren't even out there yet!" He clenched a fist and pounded the mayor's desktop. "I'd better not have lost my chance at that object while I was wasting my time here rescuing helpless colonists!"

CHAPTER 29

THOUGH FAR AWAY FROM THE BHEKAR RO BATTLE-field, Sarah Kerrigan watched the progress of Kukulkan Brood from deep within the quivering organic walls of her ever-growing hive on Char.

During the battles, she felt the loss of each one of her minions, first as the pathetic colonists fought back, then as the *Norad III* and the hated General Edmund Duke brought Alpha Squadron down to dev-astate her advancing forces. And then the protoss ground troops were fighting the zerg for possession of the xel'naga artifact.

She experienced neither pain nor sorrow for the loss of those creatures, however. They existed to be sacrificed. Zerg minions were designed to be expend-able. That didn't worry her.

However, in her progress toward replacing the full-fledged Overmind, the Queen of Blades maintained a tally of her living resources, counting each death as a number, a statistic.

With a twinge of anger, Kerrigan sent instructions to Kukulkan Brood, to the overlords and hatcheries, commanding the production of more larvae, more minions. And more. Sooner or later, in her plans for complete conquest of the galactic sector, she would need them all anyway.

And she would need the xel'naga artifact.

It infuriated her that the protoss ships had arrived and established a base at the artifact first. As her anger flowed around her, several guardians hissed and began to move up and down the tunnels, reflecting her agitation. Before they could damage the hive, which would eventually heal itself, Sarah Kerrigan calmed her thoughts and focused instead on her growing plan, developing an overall scheme of betrayal and conquest that would become an all-out Brood war—the next step in her blueprint for domination and revenge.

Seeing Alpha Squadron, Kerrigan was again reminded of Jim Raynor, a man she might have loved. Raynor had been a special terran, willing to forgive even her previous life's torment as a brainwashed telepathic ghost. Jim Raynor, however, was part of her human past—before she had fallen victim to Arcturus Mengsk's betrayal, before she joined with the zerg.

She did not resent Mengsk for bringing her together with the zerg . . . though she would personally eviscerate him and rip the self-proclaimed emperor limb from limb as soon as she captured the man. For the sheer pleasure of it.

It was only a matter of time.

Kerrigan reviewed her previous encounter with the too-confident and overblown General Duke, during their rescue operation on the *Norad II*.

She did not regret that part of her life. Instead, she remembered every detail and considered how she could use it to her advantage—to the zerg advantage.

As the war on Bhekar Ro continued, the Queen of Blades focused a small part of her expanded mind on the struggle, while devoting most of her attention to even more important matters.

CHAPTER 30

BENEATH THE CRUMBLING MOUNTAINSIDE THAT held the coveted artifact, the protoss forces battled the zerg minions on the rugged valley floor.

But while the preoccupied alien armies fought each other, the three dropships dispatched by Alpha Squadron streaked in, carrying their own infiltration squad.

Dropships were quirky vessels, difficult to maneuver and prone to mechanical failures, but the daredevil pilots flew above the echoing explosions of the battlefield. It required fancy maneuvering to ride the shock waves from the psionic storm unleashed by Executor Koronis.

The dropships had no weapons and relied primarily upon speed and their hull armor. They dodged low, moving fast, trying to reach their objective without being shot down.

Flying mutalisks, a few stragglers not directly engaged against the protoss, came after them. Splitting up, the three dropship pilots engaged in evasive maneuvers. Though the acid spray of the zerg attackers pitted and damaged their thick hulls, the ships arrived at the broken mountain range and descended to where the huge pulsing alien artifact lay exposed.

Protoss and zerg antagonists redirected their firepower, dispatching a few fighters to attack the terran interlopers. As the dropships hovered over the giant target object, the pilots knew they had little time.

Led by Lieutenant Scott from the *Norad III*, a group of marines, firebats, and four magnificently armored soldiers called goliaths hurried to the deployment doors. The goliaths looked as much like walking bipedal tanks as men. They dropped out first, their powerful armor suits absorbing the impact. Marines and thick-suited firebats spun down on rappel ropes to land on the boulders around the shimmering surface of the artifact's convoluted exterior.

"Go! Go!" shouted Lieutenant Scott, a command issued both to his men—and to the vulnerable dropships

As soon as the last marine released his rope, the first dropship wheeled about and spun upward, racing away at full acceleration. The other four dropships followed, forming a wing in the sky.

Running across the rubble, Lieutenant Scott directed his troops to the artifact's nearest opening. "Come on, let's get inside! Our orders are to map out this thing and bring back whatever reconnaissance and intelligence we can gather."

Bent low, their eight-millimeter C-14 Gauss impalers drawn and pointed ahead, the marines raced forward into the opening. The entrance looked less like a passageway than some kind of bubble in a biopolymer resin. One goliath went in with the first group, his heavy firepower ready to defend the team. The firebats hustled in next, looking for something to blast with their plasma-based Perdition flamethrowers.

As Lieutenant Scott prepared to follow, he looked up and was dismayed to see the dropships fleeing from a concerted enemy attack. Mutalisks converged on two of the quirky vessels, and though the pilots dodged and put on a fantastic show of aerial combat, the zerg attackers proved too much for them. Before long, acid cut through the engines, and the armored hulls split open.

In a last strategic move, the doomed pilots both careened into a cluster of battling alien ground troops, wiping out a handful of zerg and protoss as the two dropships exploded on impact. The last remaining dropship, though damaged, valiantly got away, flew over the low foothills, and limped back to the Free Haven base.

Lieutenant Scott followed his troops into the convoluted passageways, and it wasn't long before they encountered a firefight of their own. Inside the topmost tunnel three powerful protoss zealots loomed out at them, eyes blazing, mouthless faces giving them a demonic appearance.

"Look out!" Scott shouted.

The zealots raised their strangely gloved hands and activated deadly psionic blades. The marines were already opening fire. Their Gauss rifles sent out blasts that drove the protoss back, even as the zealots slashed with their crackling scythes.

Lieutenant Scott hadn't had time to know all the men assigned to him for this mission, so he didn't immediately recall the names of the three marines who fell screaming. While the fallen soldiers' impalers still sputtered energy bursts into the translucent wall, the lieutenant motioned one of his goliaths forward.

The goliath advanced, his armor fully powered, his twin thirty-millimeter autocannons blazing. The weapon blasted without pause until the nearest zealot toppled backward, dead.

Six firebats converged on the other two enemy fanatics. Flames erupted from their Perdition weapons. In a last struggle, one protoss zealot killed a firebat with his psionic blade, but then the flamethrowers crisped the surviving two aliens. They all fell dead next to the three marines they had slaughtered.

Scott tightened up his squad and ordered them forward, sparing only a quick glance at the martyred marines. "The clock is ticking. Let's keep moving." He knew this mission depended on momentum and speed. He could not spare any time for a ceremony that would make their fallen comrades rest more easily.

Though the lieutenant's commando team was vastly outnumbered, he planned to get them in and out, causing damage to the enemy while drawing as little attention to themselves as possible. Nobody knew exactly what this alien artifact was, but he intended to find out and return to General Duke with that information.

The team wound deeper into the object, planting locator blips so they could find their way back out again. Scott glanced at his suit chronometer to see how much time remained until their scheduled rendezvous. "Stimpacks, everyone," he called. "We need the extra boost."

Inside each marine's powered combat suit and each firebat's heavy combat suit, the in-field chemical delivery systems injected a powerful mixture of synthetic adrenaline and endorphins. Lieutenant Scott knew of the risks and potential side effects, as well as the increased unruliness caused by the psychotropic aggression-amplifier drug, but right now his team required the increased speed and reflexes the stimpacks would allow.

They charged forward, moving deeper, spiraling downward, until they encountered four massive crab-like machines. The strange alien cyborgs had four articulated claw-legs and round body cores. Dragoons!

The dragoons seemed to be on their way *out* of the artifact. Scott realized that if he had been the protoss military commander, he would have sent these cyborg warriors in as a first reconnaissance party. These dragoons might already be carrying vital information.

He knew, however, that no terran technology could ever read the alien encryption in any data-recording devices carried by the dragoons. He also knew he dared not let this intelligence fall into the hands of the protoss commander.

"Open fire!" he shouted.

Like angry spiders, the dragoons had already drawn back, preparing their phase-disrupter weapons. The goliaths activated their twin autocannons, targeting two of the four cyborg warriors. In the confined tunnels, the heavy ammunition caused more than enough destruction to take out one of the protoss cyborg warriors.

The other two dragoons, though, were able to fire their bolts of antiparticles sheathed in a psychically charged field. Two firebats, three marines, and one goliath buckled, their bodies pummeled into jelly by the force.

Shouting with anger and bloodlust, other firebats closed in. Their range was shorter than the marines' Gauss rifles, but when their Perdition flamethrowers lanced out, they concentrated on the body core until the fluid containing the alien brain began to boil.

One of the tanks exploded, spraying life-support liquid and boiled chunks of gray matter onto the corridor walls. The other dragoon fell over on its side, four legs twitching and thrashing, like a bug that had been drowned in insecticide.

Covering his mouth with a protective mask to

block the burning stench of death in the corridor, Lieutenant Scott blinked the stinging fumes from his eyes and guided the surviving members of his team forward.

"We've got a job to finish," he said. "Let's get to the core of this object and then go home to supper."

CHAPTER 31

AS SHE WORKED WITH THE WOUNDED IN FREE Haven, the tugging call in the back of Octavia's mind grew stronger. It seemed the more she ignored the mental call, the greater the tugging became, an insistent psychic pull that reached out—not to her, specifically, but to anyone who would listen.

Among the settlers on Bhekar Ro, Octavia somehow knew that because of her deep intuition she was the only one who could hear the weird call. She looked up and around, trying to pinpoint its source. The urgent summons whispered to her from the foothills on this side of the valley where alien forces were fighting over the giant artifact that had killed Lars.

This mental signal did not come from the artifact, though. It was much closer, and it . . . *sounded* different.

All around Free Haven, the marines bustled about, calling to each other, moving from duty to duty in a rapid takeover and total conversion of what had once been a quiet colonial town.

After the great battle the day before, the zerg attackers had fallen back and had not attempted any new offensives. Even the strange carpet of creeping biomass that had spread to engulf Rastin's land now seemed to have retreated. The zerg were focusing their attention on the distant valley where they fought against another group of aliens that General Duke had called protoss. The protoss had apparently sent the mechanical observer that the colonists' clunky old missile turret had shot down.

Until recently Octavia had thought her life was complicated, given the problems and difficulties she had to face daily. But now she realized the whole world of Bhekar Ro was just the tiniest blip on the vast galactic screen. Even with the zerg gone from Free Haven, Alpha Squadron wasted no time in setting up full-fledged defenses.

The SCVs made quick work of creating a heavily armored perimeter where the fence had been, using pieces from existing colony buildings as well as mineral resources they ripped from the fertile ground around the settlement. They rapidly constructed bunkers and erected missile turrets—new, functional ones. Marines and firebats filled the new facilities, while others were stationed inside the homes of some of the settlers that had not survived the zerg offensive.

Farther out, beyond the ugly erected fortifications, siege tanks patrolled the area, crushing the surviving crops, knocking down orchards for better visibility of an oncoming alien army. Massively armored goliaths strode about in search of something to fight. Vulture hover bikes cruised over the ground, acting as scouts. Their humming whine cut the air and they looked like wasps as they zipped along, crisscrossing the terrain and dropping sinister little packages called spidermines. These small robotic bombs scurried about once they hit the ground, searched for an appropriate place to bury themselves, and waited with a sensor net for the approach of heavy enemy forces.

Free Haven had become an armed camp, and the colonists were prisoners inside their own village. General Duke, broadcasting his gruff voice over powerful loudspeakers mounted on the tops of buildings around the town square, instructed all civilians to remain behind the fortifications, "for your own protection."

Mayor Nikolai made a show of complaining vigorously so the colonists could see that he was defending their interests. He chastised the general for overstepping the bounds of his authority, for damaging the settlers' hard-won agricultural land, and for devastating the meager stores they had managed to put by after forty years of eking out an existence.

General Duke and Alpha Squadron ignored him.

Trying to stay out of the general's way, Octavia felt the psychic call grow stronger in her mind. She'd already had her run-in with the commander and decided it would accomplish nothing if she argued with him. But perhaps there were other answers waiting for her, answers that surpassed anything this warmonger could comprehend.

If only she could understand what the strange mental presence was trying to tell her. She felt it was something deeply important. The answers were waiting . . . if only she could get out of here.

Later, as night fell, the colonists went back to their crowded homes. Some of them shared dwellings now to accommodate the marines stationed there. Some just wanted the comfort of more people.

Octavia, though, waited outside in the shadows, looking for her chance to sneak past the terran soldiers.

Despite their grumbling at the repressive orders of General Duke, few of the colonists would want to slip past the defensive perimeter, especially at night. The marines would be looking for a zerg attack coming toward the town. Nobody would be watching closely for someone like her, a single young woman creeping past the boundary, skirting the new missile turrets and dashing out into the night. Even if General Duke discovered that she was trying to go into the forbidden areas, he probably wouldn't deem it worth the effort to protect her against her wishes.

At the moment, Octavia did not fear the zerg. Their attack had been open and blatant. She sensed they would not crouch behind rocks in the darkness, hoping to snatch up one or two helpless victims like herself. Judging by the seismic traces of the major battle occurring at the artifact, the zerg and the protoss both had more pressing concerns.

As soon as she had accepted the tugging in her mind and moved in response to it, the call became clearer. Octavia moved across the ground, knowing this could be a trap. The mental beckoning could be a siren song luring her to her death. But she didn't think so. Why would their enemies bother? A simple colonist like her was meaningless, irrelevant to any objective the three opposing forces might have.

She hurried up the street, feeling the taut muscles in her calves and thighs. She'd been through so much stress in the past few days, had eaten little and slept even less. Even so, her body felt fully aware, fine-tuned as if the constant flow of adrenaline had given her all the nourishment she needed.

The terran military guards did not notice her as she sneaked past. The fence did not stop her. As she jogged across the rocky ground, she was most concerned about the scattered spider-mines the vultures had planted. But those devices had been set up to detect large enemy forces, heavy ground vehicles, or creatures. She hoped—prayed—that one young female tiptoeing through the chewed-up fields would go completely unnoticed by their sensor net.

Still, she ran as fast as she could.

CHAPTER 32

DESPITE ITS CLOSE QUARTERS AND CONVOLUTED passageways, the interior of the xel'naga artifact was as much a battlefield as the barren valley outside.

Directed by the overlords of Kukulkan Brood, zerg minions had split off from the main swarm and battled their way through protoss defenders. The monsters entered the maze of wormwood passages within the greenish biopolymer walls.

Protoss zealots were sent on vigorous suicide missions by Judicator Amdor while Executor Koronis bravely directed his ground troops in the main battle. Meanwhile, the surviving members of the terran commando squadron led by Lieutenant Scott pushed their way through the passages, taking images and recording intelligence data so that they could return and provide General Duke with all the tactical information he might need.

During his years of training in the marines, Scott had learned to assess a situation with just a glance.

Now, the lieutenant kept his instincts and senses tuned to their highest pitch, hour after hour. He hoped his squadron would sustain no further casualties, but knew that was a faint hope.

Although they were deep within unexplored and mysterious territory, surrounded by hostile aliens, they were still members of Alpha Squadron. Their motto had always been "First in and first out," and they had willingly accepted their assignment. Being nervous and jumpy wouldn't make them any more efficient, and Scott didn't want his men to act like . . . colonists.

The goliaths bent low, barely fitting through the corridors as they clomped forward, weapons fully charged and ready to fire. The walls of this strange construction were studded with jewels, pointed crystals, and glowing inclusions. In all his years of service on numerous Confederacy planets, Lieutenant Scott had seen plenty of odd environments and mind-numbingly strange life-forms. But he had never been anyplace like this before.

With the goliaths in the lead, the team rounded a weird rippled corner and suddenly encountered a group of zerg already hissing and raising their spiny exoskeletons in an attack posture. Six lizardlike zerglings bounded forward, followed immediately by a lurching hydralisk that bowed its carapace and extended clawed hands.

Lieutenant Scott didn't hesitate. "Open fire!"

His men were ready for the order. The firebats

rushed into the lead and opened up their Perdition flamethrowers. Gouts of fire scorched the leaping zerglings, turning them into flailing fireballs as they sprang, only to crash into the curved walls, leaving a smear of smoking organic residue.

The goliaths launched heavy firepower of their own, using their twin autocannons to cut down the hydralisk as it shot its volley of poisonous spines.

Three more marines—now no more than bloody pincushions wearing uniforms—sprawled dead. Others ran forward, howling for revenge, opening up their Gauss rifles, screaming. Lieutenant Scott raised his weapon to his armor-padded shoulder and joined the battle.

While their fury was expended on the zerglings and the hydralisk, more alien enemies moved in from behind. Through one of the slick passages came a monstrous ultralisk, a mammoth-sized beast with bony scythes that slashed from side to side, chopping through two firebats as they turned around and opened fire at it. The blast of flame didn't even make the ultralisk pause. It lumbered forward, an unstoppable juggernaut that attacked and crushed the terran opponents.

"Defensive semicircle," Scott shouted. "Now!"

The marines unloaded hundreds of rounds, never backing away a step. The two remaining goliaths, their clanking armor partially damaged by hydralisk spines, expended their high-caliber ammunition into the ultralisk's tough hide. The firebats moved into range and unleashed their flamethrowers.

In a rampage, the smoking and bleeding ultralisk stampeded forward, heedless of the cost to its own body. The beast swung the sharp, bonelike scythes that protruded from its back and slashed the three surviving firebats, one by one.

One of the last goliaths hammered the creature, firing and firing with his autocannons at point-blank range. And yet, even as the powerful blasts tore a huge hole in its body core, the mammoth zerg slashed through the body-tank armor and broke the goliath to pieces.

Lieutenant Scott watched his team being decimated, but he did not call for a retreat. He continued to pump rounds into the ultralisk as it turned toward the final, damaged goliath. But the powerful armored trooper and the last five marines poured weapons fire into the lumbering hulk until finally the monster dropped in a heap, crushing one of the wounded and moaning marines on the floor.

New silence sounded like thunder around them, and Scott stared in amazement at what had just happened. He drew a deep breath, forcing his fear away, and called on every scrap of self-confidence and training he had left. He paused just a moment to clear his mind and make his decision before his few soldiers could succumb to shock.

"Forward," he said, and did not look at his fallen troops.

Taking the lead, Lieutenant Scott marched down the strange corridor. He had orders to see what was at the bottom of this bizarre alien object.

But he was sure this mission would only get harder as he and the remnants of his commando force continued deeper inside.

CHAPTER 33

OCTAVIA HERSELF BARELY UNDERSTOOD WHERE SHE was headed. Something was calling her, drawing her. In spite of herself, she followed. The presence was alien, yes. Yet somehow she felt she could trust it—had to trust it.

And so, as the darkness deepened, she walked as if in a trance. She crossed the charred and trampled fields, the ground churned by thundering zerg claws and tentacles. Thin trees in an orchard lay strewn about like kindling, trunks shredded by angry hydralisks and ultralisks.

Broken pieces of zerg minions lay strewn about, severed limbs like legs torn from giant insects, jagged fragments of hard carapaces, even a few gutted zergling bodies, though the monstrous minions had turned on and devoured most of their wounded. Foamy slime had seeped into the ground, leaving sticky patches of mud; some spots had already dried as hard as cement.

It took her several hours to reach an isolated mineral

station in the foothills—the source of the urgent psychic plea. She stepped up, looking around, but the darkness was too great around her. Thin gauzy clouds had once again choked off the stars.

Octavia came to a rocky hill about two hundred meters high. This was the place! She climbed it slowly, steadily, picking her way over boulders, until she reached a huge sharp slab of rock jutting up from the ground like a gigantic ax blade chopping its way free of the dirt.

There she stopped. The mental voice had called her to this spot, but she saw no one—at first.

"All right, I'm here," Octavia said out loud, not knowing whether the alien presence could comprehend her language. "What do you want?" She needed to know if this stranger could help her, if it could give the settlers some way to fight off this three-way invasion—zerg, protoss, and even the terran military.

Suddenly a surprised voice spoke clearly in her mind. *But terrans have no psi powers.*

"No, we don't," Octavia answered, still aloud.

I'm glad you have come, the voice said.

Then a tall, gray-skinned creature stepped out from around the ax-blade slab of rock to get a good look at Octavia. Octavia looked back.

The face had blazing eyes but no mouth, simply bony plates that somehow gave it a superior presence. Octavia sensed that this creature was female, most likely one of the protoss aliens, but not part of the alien military forces that had landed in the far valley.

"You called me," Octavia said.

Yes . . .

"I'm Octavia Bren, a colonist. Who are you and why did you call me?"

My name is Xerana. I am a dark templar of the protoss. I have studied the signal that was sent, and I believe I know its origin. I have come to bring a warning—

"Really?" Octavia cut in. "Well, your warning's a bit late. That artifact of yours already killed my brother. Hundreds of people in my town have been killed by the zerg."

Although she could not read the change of expression on the face of this alien named Xerana, Octavia thought she detected a tone of surprise in the dark templar's thought-speech. *Truly? Your brother was . . . absorbed?* Xerana tilted her head and leaned forward as if to study Octavia more closely. *But it would have no use for terrans. You are not a part of this.*

Octavia clenched her teeth. "Well, I became a part of it when that thing disintegrated my brother."

Ah. The voice was like a breath in her mind. *I did not anticipate this.*

Octavia raised her eyebrows. "You didn't anticipate a terran answering your call, either."

Xerana's voice in Octavia's mind grew even more agitated. *I knew that my mission here would be difficult. I have come to save my people, despite their ambitions and their ignorance. When I arrived on your planet, I reached out with my mind, searching for an ally, and found one. I called out, but I did not expect that you would answer.*

Octavia marveled for a moment at the idea that she and this alien being who was so unlike herself might actually become allies, that they might share common goals.

"If you're here to save the lives of your people, and if you can help me save the lives of mine, then I am your ally. I'll do anything I can to help you." Octavia looked behind her, toward the valley where the frightened people of Free Haven huddled in the darkness, dreading another attack.

We are agreed, then. We will help one another. You must believe me when I tell you that the artifact will not attempt to harm humans unless they attempt to harm it first. It is a danger only to protoss and zerg, the children of the Xel'Naga. Octavia thought she detected a hint of sadness in the mind voice here.

A night bird flew overhead, hooting as it swooped down to snatch a blacklizard from where it prowled across a flat rock. Octavia flinched, but the bird flew off with its squirming, struggling prey. The indigenous animals of Bhekar Ro had no interest in the conflict between the three powerful races.

"So, what will you do?" she asked.

I will go to the artifact.

Octavia said, "There's another . . . *presence* there. I sensed it, sort of the same way I sensed you calling me."

The artifact spoke to you?

"Not with words. Not as you're doing. Just with *feelings*. But there's definitely something there. A computer? A mind? A recorded signal? I don't know. Just be careful."

Xerana tilted her head again and looked at Octavia from an odd angle. *You are indeed an unexpected terran, Octavia. Thank you for your concern.* She stood, her long scholar's sash flapping in the light breeze. A thin tablet with strange markings adorned her wide collar. *But my life may already be forfeit. I am compelled to tell the other protoss that they must beware. If I knew of a way, I would even warn the zerg overlords, but I doubt I could communicate directly. I must go to the artifact and command all of them to leave it. Alas, I doubt that they will listen.*

And you, in turn, must persuade your terran military that this is not their fight.

Thinking of General Duke, Octavia said, "I doubt I could get anyone to listen either. But what about the artifact? We can't avoid it forever. As long as it's here on Bhekar Ro, won't there still be a danger?"

One way or another, the artifact will be gone from your planet within a few days, Xerana said. *Until that time comes, we must both do our best to keep our people safe.* With that, the dark templar turned and vanished from sight. She just . . . winked out of view.

Octavia stood still in amazement for a moment. Then she called out, not with her voice this time, but with her mind. *Xerana?*

Yes?

It's good to have an ally.

CHAPTER 34

WITH FREE HAVEN'S PERIMETER DEFENSES IN place, General Edmund Duke felt he had done all that was necessary to keep the civilian settlers safe. The previous day, his first infiltration crew had gone inside the alien artifact, led by Lieutenant Scott. Now Duke prepared for a full military assault.

It was time for Alpha Squadron to strut its stuff.

He mobilized his battlecruisers, wraiths, dropships, Arclite siege tanks, all of the ground forces, even the vultures. The general decided to hold nothing back. He hoped he could simply charge into the fray and mop up nicely, now that the protoss and zerg had weakened each other's forces.

Ordering his troops to move out, Duke himself remained at the command center in the mayor's former house. Scratching his chin, he watched the reconnaissance images as his forces crossed the boundary line of foothills and plunged into the beleaguered valley battlefield.

The assault began with a phalanx of marines and firebats who entered the middle of the war zone, flanked by the awesome power of Alpha Squadron's siege tanks. The tanks did not waste time by going into siege mode, which would have allowed them to use shock cannons for long-range attacks. Instead, the tanks simply pounded any aliens that moved.

Pushing forward relentlessly, the marines and firebats swept aside all enemy resistance, sliding through the combat area like a hot knife through congealed salt-pudding. The terran ground troops picked up speed, pushing forward with enthusiasm, glad to leave behind their long and boring tour of duty, during which they had done little but map out abandoned worlds and survey asteroid belts for resources. The men of Alpha Squadron had been eager to do some damage to the alien scum.

Watching via view-screen, General Duke clapped his hands in exhilaration. A knock came at his door, and one of the low-ranking marine guards let the civilian Octavia Bren enter. The general took one look at the young settler and said, "Can't you see I'm busy, girl? I'm directing a battle here."

"Yes, General. But I've got some information you might need to know."

He frowned, not sure that this dirt-scraper could possibly have learned anything that his own people hadn't already uncovered. Impatiently he gestured her inside, but turned back to watch the battle.

The progress of the front-line troops had left what

appeared to be an irreparable hole in the protoss and zerg defenses, but the general soon saw that this was a grave miscalculation, that his excitement was a bit premature.

"No, no!" he yelled at the screen, watching the marines and the firebats advance so quickly that the ground support at the siege tanks and the heavy armored goliaths could not keep up.

Duke grabbed his communications intercom and shouted into it, hoping that his orders would be heard through the cacophony of ground combat. "Close up ranks! Fall back to the protection of—"

Spiderlike protoss dragoons marched over rocky hillocks, approaching the rear of the exposed ground troops. In front of them, fiery-eyed zealots powered up their destructive psionic blades and charged toward the marines, trapping the ground troops. Dragoons and zealots fell upon the marines and firebats from three different directions. Even though flamethrowers and Gauss rifles sent a blizzard of destruction into the air, the protoss fanatics did not stop. Dragoons mowed down the terran infantry, and zealots waded in among them, slashing right and left, cutting the firebats and then the marines to ribbons.

"Get them some air cover! Air cover!" Duke shouted.

Belatedly, the fast wraiths streaked in, attacking from above, followed by the slower heavy battlecruisers that closed in from behind.

The marines and firebats continued to dish out destruction in self-defense, but then one of the robed protoss Templars climbed onto a pile of rocks. Raising his three-fingered hands to the sky, he summoned an awesome psionic storm that battered the wraiths into confusion, slamming the single-man fighters together, driving several down to the ground as if they had been hit by a huge invisible flyswatter.

Massively damaged, the battlecruisers and the remaining wraiths tried to pull away, but from the other side of the valley, a second High Templar called yet another psionic storm that hammered them from the east.

Only one of the battlecruisers and three wraiths managed to pull away to the relative safety of the foothills, limping back from the dangerous valley and leaving damaged and destroyed terran vessels strewn all across the battlefield.

While the Alpha Squadron battleships hovered and tried to assess their damage, a dozen hydralisks burrowed up from beneath the ground. Before the battlecruiser captain and the wraith pilots could ascend out of range, the hydralisks had lashed out with wave after wave of penetrating needle spines that pierced the battlecruiser's hull and shredded its engines. The enormous ship crashed down into the rugged foothills, while the three wraiths were turned into a confetti of metal and blood before they could even fire a shot.

"That doesn't look good, General," Octavia observed. "Shut up!" he screamed, scanning the battlefield map and trying to decide what orders to issue.

With the remaining marines and firebats cut off from the tanks and goliaths, they were caught in the middle of a bloodbath. Even as they turned their weapons on the protoss that stood against them, zerg minions closed in from the flank and fell upon them.

General Duke recognized the zerglings and guardians, but not the group of giant lumbering four-legged creatures with long canine muzzles and spiny blue fur. He had never seen anything like them. The new beasts charged in like rabid wolves, sniffing the ground, turning their eye stalks, and plunging into any weak point of the marines' defenses. General Duke had observed many types of zerg before, but these appeared to be a new form entirely.

Octavia Bren stared at the screen, shocked. "Those look like Old Blue! The aliens must have adapted something from him."

"You know where those things come from?" the general asked, turning to her sharply.

"Those aliens . . . infested a big dog at one of our outlying homesteads. That looks like what was left of him—"

"A *dog?*" Duke gave a snort of disgust. "You colonists keep *pets* around here?" He picked up his microphone, though the marines seemed to be doing everything they could, even without his direct orders. "The zerg are causing more damage, men. Concentrate your fire and take out those . . . those *Roverlisks.*"

One of the marines raised a hand in an obscene

gesture, and the General assumed he must be fending off an attack from the sky.

During the melee, eight protoss reavers slowly made their way down from the northeast, like huge armored caterpillars intent on reaching the fray. Duke knew that the marines and firebats would lose the skirmish unless they could get more air support.

Finally, the siege tanks and the towering goliaths arrived to engage the zealots and dragoons. The armored goliaths used anti-aircraft missiles to pound the four-legged cyborg walkers. One marine even came forward in heavy, powered armor and smashed open the brain case that was directing a dragoon walker.

Siege tanks beyond the range of the zealots' psionic blades pounded and pounded again. The marines and firebats never halted in their defense, and as General Duke watched, the battle changed course and finally the terran forces gained the upper hand.

For the moment.

But it didn't last long. The protoss reavers at last crawled within range and released their Scarab drones, flying bombs that zipped toward their targets and exploded. Two of the goliaths fell. A handful of marines were slaughtered in a single explosion. The tanks and goliaths were forced to turn their attention to the armored reavers. Then two carriers converged from the west, raining down a firestorm with their small, robotic interceptors.

"This isn't possible," General Duke said. "Not Alpha Squadron. Not my best forces!"

The blinding light of explosions hurt his eyes as he stared at the tactical screen. Smoke and chaos made it impossible to see any details. The ground was littered with so many fallen troops, the general could barely discern how many of his men remained alive.

The protoss carriers seemed to know exactly what to do. They concentrated their aerial attack on crushing the goliaths, and when the towering armored walkers had all been taken out, the terran siege tanks were left defenseless, like sluggish tin cans with giant targets painted on them.

General Duke could only watch as the remainder of his assault troops got trounced.

His voice was hoarse, and he spoke as if to an empty room. "It seems I have . . . greatly underestimated the alien resistance."

CHAPTER 35

IN THE HEAT OF THE BATTLE, EXECUTOR KORONIS was too involved with directing his protoss forces to notice the tiny ripple of disturbance in the air. A stranger, a hidden visitor.

Beside him, beneath the looming majesty of the naked xel'naga artifact, Judicator Amdor seethed, mentally spitting insults and fury at the zerg and terran enemies who were attempting to steal the ancient treasure. Amdor considered that the artifact belonged to him alone.

As the zealots attacked the ground forces and massive carriers flew overhead, dropping deadly squadrons of interceptors, Koronis finally sensed a cold presence—something familiar yet separate from the Khala, the psychic link that bound all protoss together. He turned, curious and troubled, just as Amdor whirled around, sensing the same thing.

In the air between them, standing on a raised mound of broken rock and scabrous dirt, a figure appeared. A tall protoss female shed a camouflage of shadows, like oil dripping off steel. She phased out of invisibility, bending light around her.

"A dark templar!" Judicator Amdor reeled, his face and mind squirming with revulsion and disgust. "Foul heretic!" His psychic shout attracted the attention of other judicators and High Templar nearby.

The female dark templar did not flinch from the insult and mental onslaught. "I come bearing a warning for you, for all the protoss here," she said. "I am Xerana, loyal to the First Born despite the persecution that judicators like you have inflicted upon us." The sinewy gray-skinned female looked squarely at Amdor, who drew himself taller, as if wishing he had a powerful weapon in his hands.

Uneasy, knowing the terrible powers the dark templar could use, Executor Koronis signaled for backup troops. He did not hate the dark templar, as Amdor did, but he was cautious, especially in this battlefield crisis.

Four zealots bounded to his aid, psionic blades already activated and flashing. One dragoon turned on its four legs and scuttled toward where the commanders had stood.

"You do not understand what you are doing," Xerana said, looking to Koronis for understanding. "You have no inkling of the true origin and purpose behind this artifact. You must not interfere with the plans of the Wanderers from Afar. Leave here."

"We are the First Born of the Xel'Naga!" Amdor

said. "You and your traitorous followers have broken from the Khala and turned renegade to our race. You have caused enough damage already. Do not intrude in this place."

Executor Koronis, though, was more interested in what could have drawn this fugitive into the den of her mortal enemies. She must have known the judicators would want to punish her. "Dark templar, what information do you have for us?"

Amdor glared at him, eyes blazing. "Executor, surely you don't mean to listen to the corrupted words of this—"

Koronis raised his three-fingered hand. "I am the commander of this protoss force. I would be a fool to dismiss any vital intelligence, regardless of its source."

Xerana leaned closer to the executor, dismissing Amdor and infuriating him further. "I have a message and a dire warning. This . . . object" —she swept her hand upward to indicate the towering face of the mysterious exposed structure—"is very dangerous. It was created by the Xel'Naga, as you have guessed, and was designed to be more powerful than either the protoss race or the zerg. Beware what you would awaken, lest it consume all of you."

"Lies," Amdor sneered. "We are the First Born. The protoss were chosen by the Xel'Naga—"

"And abandoned by them," Xerana cut in. "We did not meet their expectations. The xel'naga made other attempts to create a perfect race. The zerg were the most destructive and successful of their new breeds, but the ancient race began many experiments and kept many secrets."

"Then what do you expect us to do?" Koronis said as the battle continued to rage behind them. The dragoon and the zealots pressed closer to Xerana, waiting for orders. "Should we let the enemies have it?"

"You must leave this object alone," she said. "Everyone, of all races. Together, protoss and zerg are in the process of awakening a great peril. You must retreat, pull your forces back. You take a great risk by toying with things you do not understand."

Koronis blinked his glowing eyes in disbelief, and Amdor looked momentarily amused. Then he mentally sent loud orders. "Seize this heretic!" Waves of hatred and revulsion emanated from the judicator.

The dragoon and zealots surrounded Xerana. The dark templar scholar stood silent, deeply disappointed that her own people refused to listen to her message.

"It was *your* foul brethren who corrupted noble Tassadar!" Amdor growled. "The dark templar were the ones who opened doorways into the Void, luring other protoss away from the Khala."

Even as she was taken prisoner, Xerana did not struggle. The judicator proudly turned to Koronis. "We will soon take possession of this artifact, Executor. And with this dark templar heretic held captive aboard the *Qel'Ha,* our great expedition has changed from complete failure to a glorious victory."

CHAPTER 36

PURSUED THROUGH THE ARTIFACT'S WINDING, creepy channels, Lieutenant Scott led his few remaining marines and firebats deeper toward the mysterious core. Though the larger battle continued to rage out on the valley floor, here inside the terran commandos encountered numerous exploratory parties of protoss zealots and zerg minions, all of which seemed to have received the same reconnaissance mission as Scott's team.

It seems to be a race, he thought. *And we intend to win it.*

The light within the walls became brighter, as if some inner fire were being stoked. The jewel clusters grew larger inside the curved biopolymer structure, deep crimson gems cut in strange facets and unusual shapes, as if they were internal organs.

Scott had no idea what they would find when they reached their destination, but he doubted the zerg or the protoss knew any more than the terrans did. He would secure the information for General Duke and, if possible, prevent any aliens from acquiring the same data.

They did not pause to fight a group of zerg that slithered and clattered through the hallways. Instead the lieutenant directed his men to sprint ahead, dodging through corridors even though they heard monsters in continued pursuit. The marines and firebats were willing to keep fighting, but their bloodlust had been dampened by the severe losses their troops had already suffered. Now they preferred to complete their objective and get back out alive.

The commandos followed the glowing light ahead, descending and curving, remembering to plant "breadcrumb" locators as they raced along so they could find their way back out. Scott hoped the dropships would be there in time to pick them up. He didn't worry about that, though. The members of Alpha Squadron knew their own duties.

The throbbing light in the walls formed a hypnotic call, like a flame that drew moths out of the darkness. The zerg and the protoss seemed to feel the call as well. They followed different passages, but all of them converged toward the central mass as if every creature could find answers here.

Finally, with his marines and firebats rushing ahead, Lieutenant Scott and his squad emerged into the artifact's blazing core, an awesome, gigantic grotto filled with a light like a blazing sun. But the fire was cold and electric, and somehow *alive*.

The walls and ceiling of the grotto reflected the

light in dazzling rainbows. Jagged crystalline shards protruded in all directions. Scott stood with his mouth open, transfixed by the grandeur and the sheer power in front of him. But though he had arrived here as ordered, he had no way to explain what he saw, could not begin to draw conclusions or provide any briefing that would be at all helpful to the general.

From other passages, dark bubbly openings in the organic resin walls, zerg and protoss emerged, monstrous hydralisks and heavily armored zealots. But as they all converged in the grotto, none of the alien enemies made any move to attack. The fiery core of the xel'naga artifact was too awe-inspiring, and all three species stood stunned and amazed.

Then the heart-glow grew brighter, as if some sort of ignition had been triggered. Tentacles of light rocketed out, reflecting like lightning from the jagged Khaydarin crystals in the walls, crackling arcs all around the grotto.

One of the firebats screamed. Lieutenant Scott knew he should call for a retreat, but could not bring himself to form words. His feet were fastened to the floor, his muscles locked in position.

The energy bolts grew more powerful. The pulsing heart of the xel'naga artifact blazed into a blinding white ball. Suddenly the lightning struck out, targeting each of the life-forms within reach.

The bolts crashed into the firebats and the marines, while at the same time obliterating the zerg and protoss spectators. Lieutenant Scott opened his mouth to shout, but the energy washed over him, too, as if it was scanning and absorbing every intruder. He watched the zerg disappear, uploaded and erased. Soon everything in the grotto was wiped clean—the protoss, the zerg, and all of his squad.

Then all vision winked out of his eyes . . .

The grotto was empty of life-forms; the xel'naga thing had gathered every specimen within reach. The terrans were not necessary, but the rest of these children of the xel'naga were exactly what the artifact needed.

In all the chambers and the walls, the glowing light increased to a living blaze. Jewel clusters exploded with the surge of energy. More dirt and rocks fell from the mountainside as a vibrating hum penetrated the biopolymer skeleton.

Powering up, the long-buried xel'naga artifact at last began final preparations for its emergence . . .

CHAPTER 37

AFTER WATCHING HIS FORCES BE COMPLETELY defeated—defeated!—General Edmund Duke was in no mood to listen to panicked rumors from an untrained, dirt-streaked colonial woman. But Octavia Bren insisted on being heard. She told the general about her encounter with the dark templar Xerana, a mysterious protoss scholar who brought urgent warnings about the ancient artifact.

Not that Duke could do anything about it. How did she want him to deal with it? He had just watched his best-planned offensive get stomped into a list of casualties too long to fit on a dozen computer screens. At least now, though, he had a bit more information . . . enough to make him deeply nervous.

When Alpha Squadron had arrived here after tracking down that alien signal and the colonists' call for help, the general had assumed the exposed artifact was just another BDO—a Big Dumb Object—not particularly worth losing terran lives over, unless he had

orders to do so. Weird artifacts and mysterious structures often turned up on backwater worlds, but they
usually didn't amount to anything.

In this case, though, it was clear the zerg and the
protoss wanted possession of the artifact in the worst
way—and Duke no longer had the firepower to capture it for Emperor Arcturus Mengsk.

In his professional military opinion, that was *bad.*

"Thank you for your assessment, ma'am," he
growled, then opened a troop communication link. "I
know exactly how to respond to the situation. Call in
our best ghost. I believe MacGregor Golding will do.
Send him to me right away." He looked up to see that
the distraught settler remained standing in his office.
"Is there anything else, Miz Brown?"

"*Bren,*" she said. "My name is Octavia Bren."

Duke scowled, wondering what possible difference
this civilian's name could make in the grand scheme
of things. "If it's not tactical information, ma'am, it's
irrelevant. Now, if you'll excuse me, I have a war to
win. Not easy to pluck victory from the jaws of
defeat."

Before Octavia could leave, the door to Mayor Nik's
commandeered quarters popped open and a slender,
armor-clad man walked in. His small face appeared
streetwise, and his overlarge brown eyes above high
cheekbones looked incredibly old, as if the young
man had already seen enough to make him weary of
the entire universe. MacGregor Golding stood silent,
waiting for the general to speak. Then, as if a nagging

distraction tugged at him, the young man turned to Octavia.

Octavia felt as if she were under a high-powered scan beam. Inside the contours of her brain, she sensed a creeping telepathic presence, like a vandal ransacking her house.

"Never mind the civilian, Agent Golding," General Duke said, breaking Octavia's concentration.

The ghost turned back to the general. "But she is definitely worth a second look, sir. I was quarantined by the Confederate government and trained to channel my psionic energies. I can recognize the talent. This woman here has a great deal of natural potential. She might make a good ghost herself."

Octavia's skin crawled. "Not on your life," she said. In the brief mental link they had shared, Octavia sensed what this man, this MacGregor Golding, had been bred and trained to do. She had also gained some insight into what the commander of Alpha Squadron had in mind.

"Agent Golding," the general said. "Command decision. We originally wanted to acquire this artifact for the terran arsenal. However, given recent events, I must admit that is not likely to happen. Therefore, I have no recourse but to activate Plan B."

"Yes, General," the ghost said. *"Plan B.* Far worse than simply losing this skirmish would be to allow this object—whatever it is—to fall into the vile hands of the despicable zerg or protoss. Given the choice, we must ensure that no one has access to it."

The ghost stood at the ready in his polished hostile environment suit, packing his long C-10 canister rifle. "I'm equipped with a personal cloaking device, sir. A dropship can take me to the fringe of the battle-field, and I'll make my way in from there to paint a target."

General Duke nodded, folding his hands over the mayor's now spotlessly clean desk. "Got a battlecruiser in the high atmosphere, ready to deploy a full com-plement of warheads."

Now Octavia raged at them both for the calm and dismissive manner in which they discussed destruc-tion of such magnitude. "You can't nuke Bhekar Ro! It's *our* colony world. This is our home, where we've worked and sweated and—"

General Duke motioned for marine guards to remove her from his office. Livid, Octavia thrashed and struggled. He looked at her with open disap-proval.

"Would you rather have me lose the battle, Miz Brown?" he asked as if the answer were self-evident.

CHAPTER 38

FOR YEARS, THE DRIVING GOAL OF JUDICATOR Amdor had been to hunt down and capture one of the dark templar heretics. Their beliefs and practices were abhorrent to him, and the very knowledge of their shadowy existence, running and hiding throughout the Void, made him feel psychically ill.

For a loyal judicator, this passion took precedence over discovering xel'naga artifacts. Amdor wanted to stamp out the traitors who had led so many other protoss away from the psychic link of the Khala. The protoss were already failures in the eyes of the Xel'Naga, but they had learned to cooperate, to draw their minds together in a graceful, flowing stream of thought that bound the race into a single unit.

Except for the members of the dark templar, rebels who insisted on being independent. They tried to draw protoss minds *away*, weakening the Khala by destroying the unity of the First Born. With his every breath, Amdor felt the need to prevent such damage from continuing.

Now this loathsome female, Xerana, had willingly surrendered herself, appearing before them in the midst of their greatest battle. Amdor wished he had time to perform a full inquisition back aboard the *Qel'Ha*.

Even held captive, though, Xerana did not seem frightened. Instead, she produced images, hauling out blasphemous scrolls filled with archaic writing. "You must look at my proof," she said, her thoughts directed toward Amdor and Executor Koronis with enough mental volume that all the others could hear her. She held up a tattered scrap of a recovered document. "See the evidence for yourselves. Before you do anything foolish, you must understand what the xel'naga have left behind on this world. Do not awaken the seed."

Behind her, the curling porous walls of the luminous green object glowed brighter from the mountainside, as if some buried furnace were already heating up.

Amdor snatched the fragment out of her three-fingered hand and tore it to shreds. "We have no interest in your lies. I don't know what dark templar trick you're trying to employ. Are you calling other heretics here to help you use this great treasure in your efforts to destroy the Khala?"

Facing him squarely, Xerana gazed calmly at him. "The dark templar have no interest in destroying the

Khala. That has never been the case. Nor have *you* ever been interested in understanding *us*. First the judicators ordered the extermination of our tribe because we were an embarrassment to you. Then, when valiant protoss refused to commit such genocide, you ordered us banished, to hide us from the rest of the First Born. You drove us all from our homes, yet here I am, risking myself to warn you of the folly of what you are doing."

Xerana raised a hand to gesture toward the weird unburied object. "Do not enter this artifact. You fail to understand its nature. It is not what you think."

Judicator Amdor just sneered. "More than anything else, you have just convinced me that *I personally* must go inside and investigate." He shot a blazing-eyed glance over at Koronis. "Accompanied by the executor, of course. We shall decide for ourselves what to do with this treasure and claim its mysteries for the good of the Khala—not for outcasts like yourself."

Goaded by the fanatical judicator's challenging look, Executor Koronis had no choice but to agree.

Her shoulders sagging, Xerana hung her head, knowing she had failed. She had not really expected a different outcome. She had been morally bound to deliver her warning, to do her best to avert the potential disaster.

"In the midst of this battle, the heretic is too dangerous to hold," Amdor said. The judicator called forth zealots and dragoons and had them prepare their weapons. "All dark templar have been already judged, their lives deemed forfeit. They have turned to the lure of the Void and ignored the call of the Khala." He made a decisive gesture. "Execute this one while Executor Koronis and I enter the glorious artifact ourselves."

He moved to stand beside Koronis. The huge glowing structure seemed to call out to them, luring them closer. In his heart, Amdor felt an urgent need to go deep within its passages and experience the awe and wonder for himself.

Xerana turned a look of profound disappointment on Koronis. "You understand so little, yet you command so much."

Then, disgusted, she called upon the energies of the Void and freed herself. Using mysterious powers that she had developed during her own search through the wildness of space, Xerana reached into the all-connecting stream of Khala, the mental link that bound all protoss into a harmonious unit with different personalities but one linked psyche. Not harming them—for no dark templar ever wished to hurt one of their fellow protoss—Xerana erected temporary invisible dams in the stream of the Khala. She cut off the executor, the judicator, and all the nearby protoss forces. Xerana knew how much chaos her efforts would cause.

Severed from their precious Khala network, the protoss felt abandoned . . . alone . . . terrified. Some of the zealots wailed in telepathic voices. The closest dragoon staggered, unable to control his cyborg body anymore.

Judicator Amdor fell to his knees and raised clawed hands as if he could physically draw down threads of the Khala from the air. "I'm blind! I'm lost!"

Then, using the trick that had brought her into their midst, Xerana bent the shadows around her, folding light so that she vanished from view. In the ensuing confusion, she fled the battlefield, leaving her people to the fate dictated by their own misguided choices.

She had a long distance to run so that she wouldn't be trapped within the holocaust.

CHAPTER 39

THE TERRAN DROPSHIP FLEW LOW FROM THE BASE at the town of Free Haven and cruised over the barrier ridge. After dancing across the edge of the tumultuous battlefield, it paused just long enough, like a hummingbird dipping into nectar, then streaked away before the enemy alien forces could fire upon it.

It left a ghost behind.

MacGregor Golding, wearing his special cloak-impregnated armor, touched lightly to the ground and raced along in a camouflage of wind and shadows. The fury and destruction of the zerg and protoss fighting forces kept the alien armies so occupied that Golding could have been carrying neon flags and they would have dismissed him.

The ghost sprinted, his muscles pumped up by two full doses of Stimpacks he had secretly taken from marine stores—much more than the recommended dosage, but it was well within the limits of what his tortured body had endured through years of training locked away in Confederacy isolation. MacGregor Golding's life had been shaped and pounded until he was a living, walking weapon, a psychic bomb who now fulfilled his life's purpose—his destiny.

If a weapon could have a destiny, that is.

As Golding traversed the edge of the battlefield, he saw the carnage that remained of the victims of Alpha Squadron. Siege tanks lay blasted open, marines and firebats—or at least their body parts—lay strewn in the blood and mud of the valley floor among blackened craters and broken rocks.

Brooding knots of clouds thickened in the skies, providing cover from long-range aerial attacks. A storm would be building. The ghost could see that. From his brief contact with the telepathically susceptible mind of Octavia Bren, Golding had stolen memories of Bhekar Ro's massive storms with their laser-lightning and sonic thunder. Not even the worst storm would wash away all the blood and carnage left here from the battle, though.

But MacGregor Golding's mission could wash it clean and sterilize the entire area.

All he had to do was call down a nuclear strike.

As he came closer to the large, ominous artifact—the focus of so much strife—the ghost could feel the pounding, building call within his skull. Another gigantic telepathic presence, a powerful sleeping entity that seemed vast enough to overwhelm all of the puny life-forms that were fighting below it.

The ghost didn't know what this thing was, and

though his usual job was to gather intelligence and to infiltrate when necessary, that was not his mission now. General Duke had issued orders, and the ghost wasn't required to understand, just to carry out the objective.

This artifact must be destroyed.

The concentrations of fighters and cloak-penetrating sensors near the cliffside forced MacGregor Golding to pause. They blocked his every line of approach. He saw a large caterpillarlike reaver accompanied by an observer overhead. Those protoss devices could detect his presence and prevent him from coming closer. He shouldered his C-10 canister rifle, lightweight but bulky like a bazooka. Golding had prepared ahead, substituting some of the high-explosive rounds with special Lockdown rounds. He had a feeling they would prove extremely useful right now.

Still invisible, surrounded by the cloaking field that kept him free of casual observation, he chose his route carefully, gauging how fast he could run and what the clearest path would be. He would worry about a rapid retreat afterward. Then the ghost lowered the canister rifle and launched his Lockdown round.

He watched the arcing plume of fire and smoke travel beyond the range of his personal cloaking field. Several of the protoss and zerg looked up, but it was too late. The Lockdown round detonated, spraying the area with a dampening field that disabled the nearest reaver. The massive unit ground to a helpless halt, its weapons systems no longer functional, its powered hatches sealed so that the protoss fighters inside could not boil out and fight hand to hand.

Moving fast now, he fired a second round, and the observer overhead crashed, its sensors offline. Knowing he was safe in his invisibility now, MacGregor Golding raced ahead through the chaos, dodging zerg minions and angry protoss. They could not see a ghost.

At the sudden unexpected loss of protoss mechanized firepower, zerg minions surged forward, directed by Kukulkan Brood's overlords to take advantage of the flaw in the protoss defenses. MacGregor ran ahead, approaching the shimmering artifact, while behind him the vicious hydralisks, guardians, and zerglings plunged into the protoss with wild abandon.

Using the chaos to his benefit, intent only on his mission, on the pinnacle of his existence, the ghost took up his position and powered up his special frequency-targeting laser.

Via an encoded communications link, he contacted General Duke. "All ready, sir. I'm in position. Preparing to paint the target now."

"You may proceed, Golding. Good work," the general said. "If you don't make it out in time, I'll see that you receive full commendations. Unfortunately, they'll have to be sealed in your classified personnel file."

"Of course, General. I understand."

Golding activated the laser and marked a target on the face of the giant artifact. The tactical nuclear warheads could come down with pinpoint accuracy, thanks to him. The objective was assured.

Overhead, one of Alpha Squadron's remaining battlecruisers opened its weapons bay doors, ready to drop the atomic missiles.

MacGregor Golding was sitting right on ground zero, but he had a few seconds to get out of the way.

He started to run.

CHAPTER 40

OCTAVIA UNDERSTOOD THE STAKES WELL ENOUGH. A nuclear attack was imminent. And if the terran military attacked the ancient alien artifact, the object itself would strike back. She had no way of knowing how many terrans—and protoss, for that matter—might die in the backlash. Octavia could not muster enough compassion to care whether the zerg swarm was wiped out or not.

General Duke had treated her as if she were a hysterical child who did not know what she was dealing with. Octavia had to admit she didn't understand enough about the situation outside in the Terran Dominion, but in this case she did know more than General Duke.

Now that her efforts to persuade him to give up his ill-advised plan had failed, Octavia knew of only one place to turn. Taking a small field rover, she drove at top speed out to the ax-blade rock where she and the dark templar Xerana had first met. Leaving the rover behind, she scrambled up the rocky slope, calling out, "Xerana! Xerana!"

There was no answering voice, of course. The dark templar could not have known Octavia would come here to speak to her.

Still, when she concentrated she felt a presence at the back of her mind. Not Xerana, though. It was more like a kind of tension, a mixture of emotions she could not begin to comprehend, all rising in a wordless scream. She could tell something powerful was about to occur.

Desperate now, Octavia blocked all other thoughts from her mind and focused all her concentration on one word: *Xerana*!

She had no idea how long she stood there, the thought pulsing through her brain—*Xerana! Xerana!*—but suddenly the dark templar scholar was there. She looked ruffled and tired.

As soon as she saw the alien woman, Octavia blurted, "Xerana, I've failed. The military wouldn't listen. There's going to be an atomic explosion. You've got to stop it."

I too have spoken with my people. They too have chosen not to listen.

A hot ball formed at the pit of Octavia's stomach. "But they could all die. You said so yourself. We've got to stop them."

Ah. But we can only offer them our knowledge. We cannot make their choices for them. Their greed and prejudice have killed their common sense. What comes after . . . is of their own doing.

"But the Free Haven colonists shouldn't have to die because of someone else's stupidity," Octavia said.

No. The dark templar closed her blazing gemfire eyes, as if she were concentrating on a single deep thought.

Just then, Octavia felt that other presence again at the back of her mind, wiping out all hope of other thought or discussion. She pressed her hands to her temples as the telepathic shout grew and grew.

They were already too late.

CHAPTER 41

WHEN THE DARK TEMPLAR VANISHED BEFORE HIS eyes—escaped!—Judicator Amdor was furious. He had lost the captive he had wanted tortured, interrogated, and then executed. All of the heretics must be made into examples for the rest of the protoss race, to keep their faith in the Khala strong.

But Xerana had used foul Void powers, tapping into forbidden dark resources that were an affront to all loyal zealots, judicators, and High Templar. Amdor could not allow it to seem that she was stronger.

After the dark templar scholar fled, her mind-scrambling corruption had faded. But while mentally blinded, Amdor had never seen his rigorous followers so frightened or confused. Not even the zerg attacks had caused as much disruption and dismay as being cut off from the gentle communal flow of the Khala.

He turned to Executor Koronis, whose thoughts were carefully masked. Amdor had the strange suspi-

cion that the calm commander was as much amused
by the judicator's discomfiture as by the dark templar's
escape.

Amdor made up his mind. "I will not allow this
traitor and heretic to sway me from going inside the
xel'naga treasure. Enough ground troops and survey
teams—I will go myself. Your dragoons never
returned, nor did any of our zealot scouts. The time
has come to investigate this matter personally. Will
you come with me?"

To his surprise, Koronis declined. "I wish I could
accompany you, Judicator, but the requirements of
strategy and military duty dictate that I stay here to
direct our battle."

Amdor looked at him for a moment, as if sneering,
then accepted. "You are not worthy to walk in the
shadow of the Xel'Naga. I will shoulder the responsi-
bility for the enclave, and for the entire protoss race."

The proud judicator climbed the slope, leaving
Koronis behind to reorganize his troops and shore up
a line of defense where a mysterious lockdown deto-
nation had just wiped out all of the protoss mechanized firepower. Zerg minions were flooding into the
breach, pressing their advantage. Giving mental com-
mands, Koronis ordered more reavers to close the
gap and a carrier to strike from the sky with flying
interceptors . . .

Judicator Amdor reached the opening of the artifact
and sensed the pulsing presence inside growing stronger.
The light increased, crackling like cold fire through the

smooth translucent polymer of the labyrinthine walls. He could sense the influence of the xel'naga here, an intangible mark of the creator race. Amdor was certain this legacy was meant for him.

Their fruitless search, the long wanderings of the *Qel'Ha* had been a result of Executor Koronis's indecisiveness and lack of vision. When the expeditionary fleet returned to the ruins of Aiur, Amdor would bring hope and power to the protoss race and the Conclave would reward him well.

Stepping into the tunnels, the judicator walked quickly, choosing curves and following a golden path in his mind. He could tell where the core of this object lay, the center of its power. It seemed to call him, drawing him deeper inside, and he rushed to answer the summons. The entity would reveal everything he had ever wanted to know about the Xel'Naga.

Oddly, despite the throbbing pulse in his mind, Amdor found the artifact to be empty and silent, as if all the other infiltrators—the protoss zealots, terran commandos, and zerg invaders alike—had somehow gone away. But Amdor felt no threat in this, only a gladness that his way would not be hindered.

When at last he entered the grotto of the arctic-cold fire, it swelled and grew, drawing energy, licking the swirled sides of the cavern. Amdor stopped, and all the amazed thoughts in his mind drained away. He could no longer feel the Khala, but this *presence* was greater than even the combined mental power of the protoss race. This was magnificent.

This was *everything*.

As he stood in front of the blazing, living heart of the artifact, Amdor could put no words to his astonishment. Then inside his head, piercing through even the awakening, utterly ancient presence of this thing, he heard the hated psi-voice of the dark templar, whispering to him from a distance: "Now you will believe, Judicator. This is only the beginning. This artifact is another creation of the Xel'Naga. It knows that we are all interconnected, part of the great tapestry. And the xel'naga plan requires all of us here, every scrap of our DNA. Their legacy needs only the energy to escape."

Amdor whirled to see if Xerana had somehow followed him inside, if she dared taint this holy place with her foul presence. But the scholar was not there, only her voice. She herself had fled to safety. "You should have listened to me, Judicator Amdor."

Then she fell silent in his head, and he looked once again toward the shimmering core, which even now blazed brighter, focusing on him, assessing him—then lunging out for him.

Brilliant bolts shot in all directions, lacing the grotto with a fiery webwork of connections, forming the final pattern as it disintegrated the judicator and absorbed the last scraps of information that it needed for its full awakening.

CHAPTER 42

FOLLOWING THE BRIGHT PATH PAINTED ONTO THE surface of the artifact by the ghost's special laser, the tactical nuclear warheads plunged down through the hazy storm-breeding skies of Bhekar Ro. They were like lightning bolts hurled from the heavens by an angry god.

The ghost, MacGregor Golding, scrambled over rock outcroppings away from the giant structure. He switched off his cloaking field and left himself exposed as all the aliens turned, some noticing him, some spotting the streaks of fire coming down from distant ships high above, some just sensing an awful doom approaching.

It was just a few tactical nukes. The GPIP (guaranteed permanent incapacitation of personnel) radius wasn't too large. A stim-charged ghost, running all out, could get to the other side of the ridge, dive down among some thick rocks, and hope the mountainside offered enough shelter.

Before leaping down through scree and boulders, Golding raised his hands as if beckoning the awesome weapons closer. He heard a hissing boom through the air and the scream of their passage, then all the warheads came down like sledgehammers on top of the glowing artifact.

He found a crack in enormous talus rocks, squeezed inside to where the shadows looked dark and cool. But even there, he had to close his eyes, and through his lids the world looked bright as day . . .

In a growing burst of light, the three tactical nukes erased the front of the mountain surrounding the artifact. A flash of spreading disintegration rippled outward.

But faster still, the awakened and hungry artifact struck, drinking deeply of the energy, absorbing it all. Within a moment—too short for any clock to measure—the outward spread of atomic annihilation halted, then was sucked inside, drawn deep into the xel'naga creation like a whirlpool of power . . .

Reeling from the sonic boom, not knowing what had just happened, Executor Koronis stood by his protoss forces, unable to believe he was still alive. He could not grasp how the artifact had responded to the nuclear attack from above, but now all the translucent biopolymer convolutions awakened in a burst of radiance.

The mountainside was gone, like unlocked chains

that had fallen away. Recharged and fully awake, the living artifact at last cracked and broke free, its substance no longer an armor-like material. Now the whole thing was charged with pulsing electrical fire, a life force.

Alive, and searching.

The zerg overlords, stunned by the unexpected atomic blast, reeled, losing control of their ravenous minions. The bristling, monstrous Roverlisks, based on the genetics of Old Blue, bounded about, tearing into their zergling cohorts. Dragonlike mutalisks flew in circles, out of control and spitting a rain of glave wurm destruction down on all frenzied fighters.

The surviving protoss judicators and zealots stood in awe, looking up at the incandescent, stirring object buried by their ancient progenitors, as if a thunderous destiny were coming down upon them.

Then the web-laced blazing shell split with crackling lightning bolts as the casing spread wider, opening up like an eggshell . . .

Or a *chrysalis*.

As Koronis stared in astonishment, feeling the thoughts of all the protoss around him swelling with terror and anticipation, his own brain reached an overload. He thought of how wonderful it had been just to take his worn shard of old Khaydarin crystal to focus his thoughts, to calm himself and meditate. But this was too much for his brain, even in the flow of the Khala, to comprehend.

The dark templar Xerana had warned them. She

had tried to explain that this object was not simply an artifact, but the seed of a living creature, another prototype race developed through the genetic machinations of the Xel'Naga. Now he and his armies, along with the zerg Minions and the terran military, had not succeeded in conquering it . . . but in *reviving* it.

With a squidlike form of incandescent energy barely held within a luminous organic skin, the real creature, a glorious being, emerged from the broken shards of its cocoon. It rose like a phoenix made of giant feathery wings, grasping tentacles, and blazing suns for eyes.

Koronis stood watching the wondrous beast. It looked unlike anything he had ever seen, and yet there was nothing *wrong* about it. The creature combined elements of terran butterfly and jellyfish and sea anemone. This being had a purity of purpose that seemed to reach a pinnacle higher than either the protoss or the zerg, which were the Xel'Naga's other primary creations.

The awakened entity moved quickly, rising out of the shattered chrysalis and hovering over the battlefield. Koronis felt as if he were a part of it. The creature sang a telepathic melody, a song written by the long-dead Xel'Naga, infused with a throbbing resonance that felt attuned to every strand of his DNA.

But Koronis sensed that he and his protoss were not here just as observers. This phoenix monster needed him, and it needed the zerg. They were resources to complete its grand metamorphosis.

The buried cocoon had been placed here aeons ago, growing, incubating, waiting . . . until now.

A typhoon of wind and carefully targeted lightning bolts flew around the rising creature like a fury, and it struck out in a kaleidoscope of color across the battle-field. The protoss and the zerg stood helpless as the Xel'Naga-spawned being flashed them all with its high-powered scanning beams, disintegrating and absorbing them, gathering up their genetics, all the thoughts and souls of these other children of the Xel'Naga. The area for miles around glowed, not with nuclear radiation, but with a seething backwash of life force.

Now more than the sum of its parts, the magnifi-cent phoenix creature rose through the sky, tearing apart clouds and turning them hot and orange. The adult life-form ascended into space, leaving behind the destruction and the shell of its chrysalis in the blasted mountainside.

On its way it encountered the few remaining Alpha Squadron battlecruisers in orbit.

Already on edge, knowing that the ground forces had been wiped out in the titanic three-way battle around the artifact, the captain of the wounded battlecruiser *Napoleon* opened fire with a blast of his Yamato gun. Seeing the dazzling creature hurtling toward him like a hurricane, he had no time—or desire—to wait for orders from General Duke down in his command center in Free Haven.

The captains of the other battlecruisers came to the

same conclusion. Yamato guns fired at the oncoming phoenix-thing, unwittingly increasing the being's biological power reservoirs. It glowed brighter, hotter . . .

And as it swept past, the newborn entity vaporized, absorbed, and digested the terran battleships, drinking their power, leaving only sparkling chunks of molten debris, which flash-froze in the cold vacuum of space.

Then it engulfed and absorbed the zerg and protoss secondary forces that had remained in reserve above the planet.

Finally sated and eager to begin its new life, the strange blazing creature departed from its aeons-long home of Bhekar Ro and soared off through the Void into the vast and unexplored gulf between the stars.

CHAPTER 43

OCTAVIA PANTED, HER LEGS TREMBLING AS SHE forced her body to keep moving. The dark templar Xerana insisted that she maintain the desperate pace. They had climbed the slope together, no longer fearing any outlying zerg infestation, because all of the aliens had drawn together into the valley war zone.

Sensing imminent danger just as they crested the ridge, though, the dark templar struck Octavia with the full force of her long arm, knocking her to the ground. Xerana ducked under a rock outcropping, sheltering herself and Octavia as a blaze of yellow-white fire lit up the sky and then faded . . . too quickly.

Your marines have dropped their bombs, the dark templar said. *But the result will not be what your commander expected.*

When the light and fire began to fade, Xerana rose to her feet with Octavia beside her, and they watched from a distance as the enormous buried chrysalis cracked open and the phoenix-being hatched out of it, rose high in the air, and minutes later swept over the distant battlefield, absorbing everything. Octavia hoped they were far enough away from all the other combatants.

Welcome to the universe, Xerana said as if to the risen creature, her mental voice tinged with awe.

Octavia's mind sensed a glorious freedom and fulfillment. She now understood the presence that had been calling her for so long, and even though she hated what this alien thing had done to her brother Lars, she could not resist the pull of complete wonder. She had never before seen anything so beautiful or so utterly pure. Her eyes ached from the too-white light as the newly born luminous beast filled the valley with its incandescence and then eagerly shot up to vanish into the skies.

Come, Xerana said. *There is more here we need to see.*

They scrambled down the rough, steep slope. The battlefield valley itself continued to throb and glow. A strange pulsing fog crawled over the ground, like a nebulous remnant of life force seeping out of the stones and soil, a mist made of diamond dust. The crown of Khaydarin crystals that had surrounded the buried artifact was now pulverized and scattered about like myriad grains of sand . . . or seeds.

The two of them reached the valley floor and moved forward together. Only minutes ago Octavia had been exhausted, but now she felt recharged, more rested and nourished than she had been in years.

She did not mind that the tall dark templar strode along at a rapid pace. Octavia bounded beside Xerana, practically running. She saw scars from the battle, the twisted wreckage of destroyed machines, but no corpses—not even any splashes of blood.

Xerana, who must have picked up her thoughts, responded. *The xel'naga hatchling took all the life it could touch, and with the energy from your military's nuclear strikes, it had more life force than it could contain. It used that energy to combine all the genetics of the zerg and protoss in order to complete its maturation. Then, on its journey outward, the new hatchling shed some of its bioenergy, leaving it here.*

Octavia bit her lip. As she looked around and saw so many wonderful things, her anger came back. "Then why did it take Lars? What possible use could that creature have for human DNA?"

Xerana seemed saddened. *Your brother was a mistake. The hatchling had no use for your terran energy. It was asleep and still young. It did not understand what it was doing.*

So . . . Lars had died simply because he had been in the wrong place.

Not consoled by this, Octavia walked deeper into the valley, noticing a small change that grew more pronounced as minutes passed. The soil seemed springy, and she saw tendrils of grass, tiny shoots sprouting everywhere. They grew so quickly that she could actually see the plants moving, bursting up through the ground as if anxious to return an exuberance of life to scarred Bhekar Ro. She knelt on the ground and plucked a flower, which blossomed in her hand into a brilliant crimson bloom with three pointed petals.

It is life, Xerana said simply. Octavia could feel it in her eyes, her skin, her mind.

The powerful diamond mist began to dissipate, thinning to reveal a clear blue sky that seemed to reach all the way to the stars. Then, in the distance, Octavia saw several figures, people standing dazed and confused out in the middle of the burgeoning meadow.

They were human.

Octavia started forward, hesitantly at first, afraid to hope. Many of them wore the uniforms of terran marines, but one was dressed in settlers' clothes, serviceable coveralls . . . just like the ones her brother had worn. Octavia caught her breath, unable to believe what she was seeing. She blinked.

Xerana explained, *For the final transformation, the embryo required the genetics of the other xel'naga children as a biological fuel. Because these terrans were not necessary, the creature must have rejected them from the DNA matrix.*

"Lars!" Octavia shouted, then rushed forward, breathless. She laughed. Her resurrected brother stood in the middle of a field of flowers that looked like a fireworks show of color across the grassy valley. He turned to see her, and his face lit up. She threw herself into Lars's arms. He looked confused at first, then hugged her tightly.

"Now this *is* interesting," he said in a bemused voice.

"I can't believe you're back!" she said. Octavia grabbed his shoulders, just staring at him. Her knees felt weak. After all she had been through, this seemed the most unbelievable.

"I never thought I'd be glad to get back to this place," Lars said. Octavia hugged him again.

The dark templar female stood alone and apart. There was nothing more for her here. She had come to see and to learn. Her warning had not been heeded, and she'd been unable to save her protoss brothers, but perhaps that was for the best. The newly awakened phoenix creature was also part of the xel'naga mystery, and Xerana was glad that she had witnessed its birth.

Without a word of farewell, the dark templar scholar wrapped herself in shadows again, vanished from sight, and made her way back to her own ship.

Perhaps she could follow the newborn creature, or search for other sleeping embryos that had been hidden by the Xel'Naga. She had many questions to answer and much to do . . . and all the Void in which to search.

CHAPTER 44

THE OBLITERATION OF KUKULKAN BROOD FELT like a wound ripped into Sarah Kerrigan's side. The sickly light pulsing from the living walls of the hive around her seemed oppressive.

It was not so much anger at a humiliating defeat or sadness at the deaths of so many of her minions. What she felt was the loss of an ambitious dream, a loss of resources.

Onlya setback . . .

So far, she had worked without rest to guide the zerg back into a ferocious force that was destined to conquer the galaxy. This mission to confiscate the xel'naga artifact had been a test for her. She had wanted to demonstrate to herself that her zerg were undefeatable, that the destruction of the Overmind had been merely a fluke. The Queen of Blades was stronger, braver, more ambitious.

Now, though, she would have to reassess her plans, redefine her goals so that the dead planet of Char blossomed into a dark flower.

The burgeoning Hives generated hordes of larvae, all of which were mutated into carefully chosen configurations, minions that would fit into an overall military strategy.

Even without Kukulkan Brood, Sarah Kerrigan still had other powerful Broods—Tiamat, Fenris, Baelrog, Surtur, Jormungand. Each one was led by a different Cerebrate. Each one had a general function in the overall zerg social structure: to command, hunt, terrorize, attack. Each one had thousands, sometimes millions of loyal zerg minions.

Some had been decimated in the recent war that had brought terrans, protoss, and zerg to the brink of oblivion. But the Queen of Blades had brought them back together again.

She decided she would not concern herself with the setback on Bhekar Ro. It did not matter. Despair was a human condition, and Sarah Kerrigan no longer considered herself human.

This was only the beginning.

Soon she would launch her Brood War.

CHAPTER 45

ACCOMPANIED BY LIEUTENANT SCOTT AND HIS surviving commandos—all of whom had also been restored in the backwash of the Phoenix-creature's birth—Octavia and Lars made their way back to Free Haven.

Inside the settlement town, General Edmund Duke seemed completely lost and alone. They found Mayor Nikolai pounding on the door of his home. "I want my office back."

A handful of marine guards continued their duties around the town, but they seemed completely bereft of goal or direction. General Duke opened the door and, ignoring the mayor, pushed past to stand out in the middle of the street.

Nik rushed back into his dwelling and began to clear the general's paraphernalia off his desk.

Alpha Squadron had been wiped out on the battle-field. Duke's battlecruisers, wraiths, and ground troops had been destroyed, some of them during the orbital battle, most in the abortive assault against the zerg and the protoss near the artifact. Now, shortly after the nuclear strike and the strange unexplained events that had occurred around the buried object, he'd lost contact with his remaining ships in space. No one answered his comm signals.

He hoped they were just scattered. Perhaps a few vessels had reported directly to Emperor Mengsk. Some might come back to search for him.

But he didn't think so.

When Octavia returned with her brother, the settlers, though beaten and in shock after the war, reacted with joy to see at least one member of their colony returned alive and well. The most joyful by far, though, was Cyn McCarthy, who ran to Lars, threw her arms around him, and burst into tears. To Octavia's surprise, Lars kissed the copper-haired young woman and proposed to her on the spot— prompting a fresh wave of happy tears.

The rest of the colonists watched in a daze. So many astonishing and terrifying things had happened to them in the last few days that they did not even question the miracles they were now seeing.

Octavia's exuberance began to awaken them. "Wait until you see the valley!" she said. "It's all fertile land now, bursting with plants. We'll be able to grow any kind of crops there. I guarantee we'll have a yield higher than anything in our colony's history. It's a new chance for us, a spot of hope. We *can* get back on our feet again."

General Duke scowled at Octavia as if she were to blame. "My military force came to rescue you and now most of them are wiped out." He shouted into the office that had, until recently, been his command center. "Mayor Nikolai, I demand that you contact the Terran Dominion and request a full extraction team, battlefield analysis, and relief for my surviving men."

The mayor poked his head out the door, looking insufferably pleased with himself. He didn't seem terribly disappointed when he said, "I'm sorry, General. All of our long-range communications systems are down. They were destroyed in the attack."

General Duke growled, as if he wanted to chew on some rocks and spit out sand. "And you don't have *any* spaceports? No star traveling technology on this rock?"

Mayor Nikolai shook his head. "We're just a fledgling colony, General. 'Simple dirt-farmers,' I think you called us."

"Clodhoppers," Octavia added. "Don't worry, I'm sure they'll come looking for you eventually."

Duke balled his fists and planted them on his hips, glaring at all the townspeople. "Well, I'm stranded here then. Now what am I supposed to do?"

"Let's be practical." Octavia reached over to the wall of one of the dwellings and picked up a long-handled hoe that was stained with zerg blood. She shoved the farming implement into the flustered general's hands. "You can start *weeding*. We've got a lot of new arable land to cultivate."

Duke spluttered and could think of no response. Octavia gave him a wry smile. "It's easy, General. Any child can show you how to do it."

With the help of Lars and Cyn, she gathered Jon, Wes, Gregor, Kiernan, Kirsten, and a few other settlers, to lead them out to the lush, revitalized valley and show them where they could plant fresh crops. Handsome young Lieutenant Scott, looking at Octavia with undisguised interest, volunteered to accompany them. He seemed happy and relieved, as if he was tired of warfare and might prefer to settle down here . . .

As the colonists worked together to pick up the pieces of their scarred world, Octavia sincerely hoped they would never draw outside attention again.

ABOUT THE AUTHOR

Gabriel Mesta is a pseudonym for the husband-and-wife team of KEVIN J. ANDERSON and REBECCA MOESTA. They have written two dozen books together and dozens more separately. They have worked in many universes, including *Star Wars*, *The X-Files*, *Star Trek*, *Titan A.E.*, and *Dune*, as well as their own original worlds.